"Admit it. You deliberately set out to get under my skin tonight, didn't you?"

Kosta trailed one finger down the line of sensitivity at the back of her neck. Annis shivered. "Didn't you?"

"Yes."

His arms went around her, hard.

"Why?" he murmured against her lips.

"I—don't know." And she didn't.

"Yes, you do." His hands were molding her body. "Chemistry. You're getting the hang of it at last."

Dear Reader,

When I was twelve I made friends one holiday with a millionaire's daughter. She wasn't spoiled. She was lonely. Loneliest, perhaps, at home.

I thought I'd forgotten her. Yet when I started to write this story, I found Annis kept reminding me. Annis, though, was lucky. Her father remarried and suddenly she had a little sister!

Two women could not be less alike. Annis is clever and quiet. Bella is bubbly and beautiful. Still, they laugh together, love each other and protect each other's back. More than friends, allies.

To such an extent, in fact, that I found Annis would not let me go until I had told Bella's story, too. It disconcerted all of us, including my editor. (Completely threw her schedule.) *The Bridesmaid's Secret*, coming next month, is the result.

I hope you enjoy these books as I much as I enjoyed writing them.

Best wishes,

Sophie Weston

Readers can visit Sophie Weston's Web site at http://www.sophie-weston.com.

THE MILLIONAIRE'S DAUGHTER
Sophie Weston

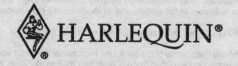

TORONTO • NEW YORK • LONDON
AMSTERDAM • PARIS • SYDNEY • HAMBURG
STOCKHOLM • ATHENS • TOKYO • MILAN • MADRID
PRAGUE • WARSAW • BUDAPEST • AUCKLAND

ISBN 0-373-03683-3

THE MILLIONAIRE'S DAUGHTER

First North American Publication 2002.

CHAPTER ONE

ANNIS CAREW walked into her father's house and stopped dead. This was not the small, family supper she had been expecting. This was a full scale dinner party with women in jewels, waiters in black tie and, inevitably, tonight's candidate to help the millionaire's plain daughter off the shelf.

And what a candidate! Annis picked him out the moment the door closed behind her. He was talking to her father on the other side of the drawing room but they both glanced up to see who had arrived. At once, Annis forgot her father, her kind matchmaking stepmother Lynda, and everyone else in the room.

The candidate was tall and good looking in a sardonic, hard edged sort of way. But it wasn't his height or his Byronic profile that stopped her breath in her throat. It was what she privately called The Look—the look of a man who did not have to try.

Annis knew The Look from grim experience. She had been meeting—and failing to make any impression on—men with The Look ever since the first smart cocktail party at which Lynda had tried to introduce her to what she called Nice People.

Oh, no, not that one, thought Annis. *Lynda, what are you trying to do to me?*

Her father had obviously been waiting for her. Lynda's instructions, no doubt. Now, as he said something to the tall dark man, he looked relieved.

Probably thought I'd realise what was going on and cut loose, thought Annis. *As I should have done. How could I be so stupid?*

On the telephone this afternoon Lynda had been casual. Too

5

casual, Annis now realised. 'Come over for supper, darling. It's so long since we've seen you,' Lynda had said.

And Annis, speeding through her flat on the way to her next meeting, had flung, 'OK. What time?' at the telephone speaker without pausing to think.

So now here she was, high and dry, an ugly duckling in her sober business suit among the swans of London's elite. Rain-draggled hair dripped down her back. Meanwhile The Look shouldered his way purposefully through the crowd to the rescue of the millionaire's plain daughter who didn't want rescuing.

Say a big hello to the perfect Friday night, thought Annis. She felt a strong urge to scream. She repressed it. Just.

Annis watched the tall figure bearing down on her. Like most of the men here this evening he was formally dressed. Unlike most of them he was wearing a high collared Nehru jacket in a muted brocade that glimmered richly in the candlelight. It skimmed his slim hips in a fashion that was as flattering as it was startling. Together with his strange, slanted eyes, it gave him an air of slightly exotic danger.

No doubt at all, thought Annis, that the effect was deliberate—and carefully calculated. A peacock, she thought, among all these high priced swans. Who on earth was he?

He reached her and took her hand.

'Across a crowded room—I knew it would happen one day.' He had a voice like black treacle, warm and deep and horribly sensuous. You could, thought Annis indignantly, probably drown in that voice. Slowly and pleasurably.

She gave him a wintry smile and removed her hand.

'Hi, doll,' said her father, arriving.

Since Annis had become a businesswoman in her own right her father treated her with a breezy camaraderie that imperfectly disguised his gratitude that she no longer admitted to emotions.

'Hi, Dad,' she said, cool as the glass of champagne a waiter was pressing into her hand.

'This is Konstantin Vitale. He specially wants to meet you.'

I'll just bet he does, thought Annis dourly. She wondered briefly whether it was the opportunity for business offered by her father's company or her own status as an heiress that had drawn Konstantin Vitale across the room to her side.

Tony Carew answered the question for her. 'He's working on the headquarters project.'

'Ah. Palazzo Carew,' said Annis, understanding.

Her father's plans for the new centre he was going to build for his company were enthusiastically extravagant. They had impressed the media and had stunned his rivals. His family had been teasing him about them for months.

'So, here's your mystery woman, Vitale.' He sounded pleased with himself 'My daughter, Annis.'

'*Mystery* woman?' echoed Annis. She was growing warier by the minute.

The Byronic hero answered before her father had the chance. 'So late. So damp. So preoccupied.'

To her annoyance, an instinctive hand flew to the soaked strands at the base of her neck. His eyes followed the gesture. She felt embarrassment heat her skin.

She said more sharply than she intended, 'Nothing mysterious about being late. I let time get away from me, that's all.'

'You two should have a lot in common,' Tony announced.

He gave Annis a conspiratorial grin before he pushed off. She knew that grin. It meant things were going to plan. In this case, she was almost certain the plan in question had been laid down in advance of the party by his wife. She ground her teeth silently.

'You don't look as if you agree with him,' said the black treacle voice, amused. But not only amused. The damned man sounded as if he was *caressing* her.

Annis felt her spine arch like an angry cat's. Over his shoulder she could see her reflection in the oval Venetian mirror. It was eighteenth century, one of Lynda's finds. Curlicued and garlanded, gleaming with gold, it might have been made for Konstantin Vitale, with his brocade coat and dramatic profile. It had certainly never been intended to reflect someone like

Annis. Her short dark hair had been turned black by the rain and was now plastered to her head like a skullcap. The only good thing about it was that the wet hair was also plastered over the ugly scar that ran from her eyebrow to her hairline. Realising it, she scowled horribly, then saw that he was laughing at her again.

Hurriedly Annis readjusted her expression.

'I always try to keep an open mind,' she said lightly.

He hardly pretended to believe her.

'Sure you do.'

Her reflected brows snapped together in a frown of irritation. Annis saw it in despair. Her frowns were notorious. There never seemed to be anything that she could do about them, either.

She struggled to forget that she was over-tired, underdressed and that her minimal make-up had run in the rain. And that the Lord Byron look-alike in front of her had noticed every detail. She even tried to hide how thoroughly jangled she was to find the promised family supper transformed into one of Lynda's find-Annis-a-man fests. After all, none of that was Konstantin Vitale's fault, she reminded herself.

'Sorry,' she said. 'Put it down to end-of-the-week neurosis.' She squared her shoulders, pinned on a polite smile, and tried to retune her mind to social conversation. 'So what does my father think we have in common?'

The sardonic expression was very evident. 'To be honest it was Mrs Carew who said you and I ought to get together.'

'Surprise me,' muttered Annis.

'Excuse me?'

She shook her head, annoyed with herself. 'Nothing.'

His eyes were speculative. 'She respects you a lot.'

But not enough to accept that I can live without a man. There was a pregnant pause while Annis closed her lips over that one.

'No, really. She's a real fan. She was telling me how smart you are. What a great stepdaughter.' It was almost a question.

Annis knew she was not reacting like a great stepdaughter. 'That was kind of her,' she managed in a stifled voice.

'And unusual.'

Quite suddenly Annis realised she had run out of the ability to pretend. It was something to do with Friday-night tiredness. But more, much more, to do with that seductive voice and the horrible feeling that she was being sucked into something she could not control.

'No,' she said on an explosive little sigh. 'No, it's not unusual. Lynda does a terrific marketing campaign.'

'What?'

She fixed the tall dark stranger with a baleful eye. She had been in this situation before. Experience told her there was only one thing she had never tried. Take a firm line straight from the start and hang on to it.

She took a deep breath and did just that. 'Look, I don't know what Lynda has told you. But let me set the record straight.'

He looked politely intrigued.

Annis drew a deep breath. 'I'm twenty-nine years old, I live for my work and I don't date.'

The man had high cheekbones and strange, slanting green eyes. They did not blink. Not blinking, he said a lot.

Ouch, Annis thought. *I don't think I meant it to sound like that.*

She added hastily, 'Nothing personal.'

It was not, perhaps, brilliantly tactful. The green eyes narrowed almost to slits.

'That's a relief,' he said with a dryness that made her wince.

The deep voice had just a hint of a foreign accent. A very sexy accent. And he was taller than she was. Annis did not usually have to look up to people. It threw her off balance in every way.

'I don't want anyone to get the wrong idea. I mean I just like to make things clear. In general.' She was floundering. *Come on, Annis, you can do better than this.* 'Sometimes Lynda can be a bit misleading...'

He did not say anything, maintaining his air of gentle interest. Annis ran out of excusing generalities.

She tried the truth. 'I—er—I mean I'm a bit of a workaholic.'

She made a despairing gesture. Too big a gesture, as always in this room of *objets d'art*. Champagne fountained from the glass she'd forgotten she was holding. At the same time a gold-painted plinth swayed at the impact. Konstantin Vitale steadied it. She saw he was looking deeply amused.

Amused! Great!

Of course, she *could* have said, My stepmother has set me up once too often. She thinks it would be nice for me to meet you. And when she says meet, she means dine with, dance with, holiday with, sleep with and, in the fullness of time, marry. Because my stepmother cannot get her head round the idea that any woman of my age might have other priorities. She thinks I'm scarred and difficult and on the shelf. She wants to help. You're just the latest in a long, long line of unattached men she thinks might be good for me.

Oh, yes, she could have said that. It was there, every furious word, seething on the tip of her tongue.

Except, Annis was realising uneasily, he did not look like the latest in a long line of anyone. Nor, on consideration, like the sort of man who was likely to be good for the woman of the moment. Challenging, exciting and unpredictable, yes; cynical, certainly. Not, good.

Annis looked into the handsome, world-weary face and was assailed by doubt. Surely even Lynda, who thought she had a moral obligation to throw unmarried people together, wouldn't imagine she could matchmake for a sophisticate like this?

She said gropingly, 'Lynda did say she wanted us to meet?'

He was straightening the abstract sculpture on the plinth she had nearly sent flying. He glanced down at her, green eyes glinting.

'Those common interests of ours, I guess.'

He looked perfectly solemn but Annis knew he was laughing.

Annis's doubts disappeared. So her first suspicions had been right after all. She was oddly disappointed. She did not *want* him to be the sort of man to date a millionaire's daughter, sight unseen.

'Oh, yes?' she said freezingly.

He was bland. 'Meet another workaholic.'

And he held out his hand again.

To her own annoyance, Annis found herself taking it as if he had mesmerised her. It was not the light, social brush of the fingers of that first handshake either. It was a purposeful grasp, as if he were giving her a message.

Startled, she looked down. His hand was tanned and strong. It looked as if he had been working outdoors somewhere in the sun. Her ringless fingers were as pale as water engulfed in his clasp, and looked about as weak, Annis thought in disgust. Was that his message? Indignant she lifted her head and glared right into those strange eyes.

There was a moment's silence.

Then, 'Yeah,' he drawled. As if she had asked him a question. Or as if she were a strange girl he was sizing up across a fairground or the floor of a nightclub. Sizing her up, what was more, with lazy appreciation.

Appreciation? Ridiculous. He had to be mocking her.

Annis tugged her hand away in pure reflex.

She half turned away and spoke at random. 'If you're a genuine workaholic, what are you doing at a party? There's at least another four hours' working time left tonight.'

It wasn't a very good joke and Konstantin Vitale didn't laugh.

'I could ask you the same thing,' he said slowly.

Annis was curt. 'Family.' She was not going to admit that her stepmother had got her here under false pretences, though. It made her look a fool. So she added lightly, 'Lynda's dinner parties are a three-line whip. Besides, I haven't seen my father since Carew's half-year results.'

Konstantin Vitale glanced across at his host, currently holding forth by the fireplace. His mouth curled.

'You work for Carew's? I thought your stepmother said you were independent.'

Annis bristled. 'I am. I still take an interest in the family firm.'

The sardonic look deepened. 'Of course. Why didn't I think of that?'

He doesn't like me, she thought. Well, that was mutual.

'Families do usually take an interest in each other's affairs.'

'I'll take your word for it,' he said dryly.

Annis narrowed her eyes at him challengingly. 'No family, Mr Vitale?'

'None that I'd discuss my financial results with.'

Annis saw the chance for revenge.

'Could this be why you're a workaholic?' she asked sweetly.

He appeared to consider the question. 'Nothing better to do with my time?' he interpreted. He shook his head decisively. 'No, it's not that. You see, unlike you, I do date.'

The riposte was so unexpected that for a moment Annis could not think of a thing to say. Then she saw the devilish glint of laughter in the green eyes. And was swamped by a blush.

Oh, boy, what a restful Friday evening this was turning out to be!

Annis tried to ignore the heat in her face and the nasty sensation that a master had beaten her at her own game.

'Each to his own,' she said crisply, preparing to turn away.

He stopped her by propping himself against the wall and barring her escape route.

'I so agree. And what is your own, Annis Carew? Are you just playing at business, propped up by family money? Is that what you're doing here? Checking that the subsidy will keep coming?'

Annis was so indignant she forgot the dying blush.

'I'm here to network,' she said furiously and quite untruthfully. 'In my line of work you seize every opportunity.'

She comforted herself that lots of management consultants

did network a great deal. Just because she and her business partner Roy did not choose to, that didn't undermine the general principle.

'Plenty of people worth networking with,' agreed Konstantin Vitale.

How did he manage to sound as if he had found a slug in his salad?

Annis conveniently ignored the fact that when she'd arrived this evening her heart had sunk at the sight of all these dauntingly impressive people. 'Lucky me,' she said brightly.

Konstantin Vitale looked bored. 'And what is this work that you live for?'

'I'm a management consultant.'

'Impressive.' His voice was grave and his face did not change by a muscle.

So why did she think he was mocking her?

Annis set her teeth and decided to fight fire with fire. 'And what to you do when you're working on my father's new building?'

He gave a soft laugh. 'I keep Carew in line.'

Annis was genuinely startled. *'What?'*

He repeated it obligingly.

Clever, she thought. Her father's friends called him Tony; his subordinates called him *Mr* Carew. Konstantin Vitale was making a point. Not an employee, then. And if he was a professional adviser, he was not a very respectful one.

Annis bristled. 'Forgive me if I say that I find it difficult to imagine.'

'Too right,' said Konstantin Vitale blandly. 'He's stubborn as hell.'

Most people who worked with Tony Carew were impressed by him. If they weren't impressed they did not last very long.

'I take it that your professional relationship with my father is on its last legs?' said Annis

He was surprised. 'No. Why? He wants the best. I am the best. He just needs a bit of education to appreciate it, that's all.'

Annis blinked. She found she had nothing to say in the face of such superb assurance. *Out of my depth again.*

'Could be it runs in the family,' he murmured provocatively.

Annis was instantly suspicious. 'What does?'

'A need to be challenged.'

She met his eyes in fulminating silence. He raised one eyebrow. He was amused, confident and—quite temporarily—ready to duel with her. Oh, that Look! Annis could have stamped her foot with frustration.

She stopped pretending that she did not know he was trying to wind her up.

'No chance,' she said curtly. 'Forget it, Mr Vitale. I not only don't date, I don't play any other silly games either. Now, I must find my stepmother. Excuse me.'

Annis was still seething when she tracked Lynda down. Her stepmother kissed her on both cheeks, all wide-eyed innocence.

'So lovely to see you, darling. I saw your father was looking after you. How did you get on with lovely Kosta?'

Annis did not answer that directly. 'He's tonight's people's choice, is he?' she said grimly.

Lynda fingered her fabulously simple, fabulously expensive gold collar nervously. She avoided Annis's eyes.

'Your father asked him. They're doing business together, I think.'

'And no doubt I'm sitting next to him at dinner.'

Her stepmother did not deny it. Another unwelcome thought occurred to Annis, based on previous experience.

'And my flat just happens to be on his way home, I suppose?'

Lynda did not deny that either. She scanned Annis's face, clearly concerned.

'Darling—'

Annis was surprised at the gust of fury that whipped through her. Konstantin Vitale had disturbed her more than any other of Lynda's offerings, though she could not have said why. She just knew that she hated it.

'So he offers to drive me home and I'm supposed to say thank you kindly. *And* go out with him when he calls next week.' She was shaking with anger. 'Tell me, Lynda, have you given him my number already?'

In spite of a designer cocktail suit and several thousand pounds' worth of discreet jewellery, Lynda Carew looked like a guilty four year old caught out in the playground.

'Not to Kosta. But darling—'

'Lynda, I love you very much. But will you just stop interfering in my life?'

Lynda looked shaken. Annis had never reacted like this before. All right, she did not usually go out with the men Lynda introduced to her more than once. But at least she greeted them with amused resignation. Lynda had never seen such passion in her level-headed stepdaughter. Or not about men.

She tried to sound airy. 'But your father had these business types he really wanted to invite. So I thought, Why not?' Her eyes were huge, blue and limpid. 'Starting out on her own like that, Annis will probably be glad of a chance to meet some people who could put work her way.'

Annis stared. It was so close to what she had already claimed herself that Lynda might have been eavesdropping. *Hoist with my own petard*, she thought. In spite of herself, her lips twitched. She flung up her hands in surrender.

'OK. I'm here to network. Let's leave it at that.' But she still looked at Lynda severely. 'And I get to go home alone, right?'

'Right,' said Lynda relieved. She patted Annis's sober blue shoulder. 'I suppose you've come straight from work?'

Annis sipped the champagne. 'How did you guess?'

'You're always scratchy when you're tired,' Lynda said frankly.

That was undoubtedly true. Annis, always fair minded, had to admit it.

Lynda sensed a softening. 'I wish you wouldn't make things

so difficult for yourself, darling. Why don't you just try to enjoy yourself for once?'

Annis closed her eyes briefly. 'You've been saying that since I was fourteen.'

'Then, it's about time you gave it a try.'

Annis opened her mouth to retort.

'What you ought to do is go upstairs to my room and freshen up,' Lynda said coaxingly. 'That will make you feel better. Borrow an earring or something. And then come downstairs and be *nice* to people.'

There was a shout of loud laughter from her father's group at the fireplace. Lynda put a hand on her Annis's arm. Her expression was suddenly serious.

'Don't spoil it, Annis,' she said in a low voice. 'It's so long since he relaxed properly.'

Annis looked down from her five feet eleven into her diminutive stepmother's exquisite face. Annis had given thanks for Lynda every day since she'd married Tony Carew and had taken his daughter under her wing. They were as different as two women could be but Lynda had given her unstinting affection, making no distinction between Annis and her own daughter Isabella.

What was more, she made Tony Carew laugh again. Under Lynda's influence he came home from the office at night. He even took some notice of his neglected ugly duckling daughter and found, to his astonishment, that she was interesting. Found that she was not a sullen adolescent, just painfully shy. Found that he liked her.

So now Annis looked at Lynda, who would not remind her that it was she who had given Annis back her father. Annis knew herself beaten. Again.

'Yes,' she said capitulating entirely. 'Yes, all right. I'll paint my face and sing for my supper. Just no more throwing me together with your spare men.'

Lynda laughed and let go of her arm. 'Take your drink with you.'

It was only when Annis was sitting in front of her step-

mother's enormous dressing table that she realised that Lynda
had made no promises.

'Outsmarted again,' she told her reflection with irony, and,
as she so often ended up saying after a tussle of wills with
her sweetly accommodating stepmother, 'When will you
learn? You'll walk straight back into the arms of tonight's Mr
Available.'

Only, in spite of all the evidence to the contrary, Konstantin
Vitale did not feel like Mr Available. Reflecting on that
exchange downstairs, her eyebrows knit in puzzlement.

Of course, it was probably not his fault. It was even possible
that he did not know that Lynda was matchmaking. Annis
knew her stepmother very well. The most Lynda would have
told him was that she needed a spare man to make up numbers
and sit next to her clever stepdaughter. That's what she had
told the sculptor, the writer and the aspiring politician.

Lynda's candidates were normally men with promising fu-
tures and a shortage of current cash. That was what made the
idea of dating millionaire Tony Carew's daughter rather attractive, no matter how scarred and difficult she might turn
out to be. Annis wondered exactly what Konstantin Vitale did
for a living. And if she had done enough to make him think
better of the dating-the-unattractive-heiress scenario.

Annis found her reflection was frowning horribly. She
leaned forward and smoothed her heavy eyebrows apart.
'Borrow an earring,' Lynda had said. Well, she could do better
than that with the run of her stepmother's resources. With the
efficiency of long, long practice, Annis set about livening up
her neat navy business suit.

She borrowed a silk scarf so fine that it was transparent,
with the evening colours of an impressionist painting shimmering as she moved, and some long turquoise earrings that
Lynda had brought back from Morocco. No time for elaborate
make-up, thought Annis, who was no good at it, even at the
best of times. So she just combed her hair forward to hide the
scar, flicked damp fronds into place against her long neck and
dusted a touch of rose to her full-lipped mouth.

Then she squared her shoulders and went back to face the battle.

Fortunately the first person she saw was not Konstantin Vitale. Not even another glamorous spare man. It was Lynda's own daughter, Bella.

Isabella, at twenty-three as golden and charming as her mother, regarded Annis as one of her very best friends.

It was Bella who saved her now.

'Annie,' she screamed, rushing over.

A number of people looked up and smiled. Across the room, Annis saw, even Konstantin Vitale of The Look glanced up. For a moment the bored shell cracked. He looked almost intrigued. But then, thought Annis wryly, men usually did look intrigued when they first caught sight of Isabella Carew.

Tonight she was on top form, in a slip of a dress that was all shimmery curves and slipping straps, showing yards of perfect leg. She enveloped Annis in a bear hug.

'Hi, Brain Box.'

Annis kissed her sister more sedately. 'Hi yourself, Bella Bug. How's life?'

'Great. What—'

Lynda frowned her daughter down. 'We can have a family chat later. There's someone I want Annis to meet.'

'*Another* one?' said Annis incredulously.

Bella grinned. She was not hampered by any chivalrous feelings of obligation and she knew as well as Annis did what Lynda was up to. Only Bella was a lot better at heading off her mother's matchmaking tactics.

'Leave it out, Mother. The girl works. She's had a hard day. Let her get her breath before Prince Charming parachutes in.'

Annoyance tightened Lynda's pretty mouth for a moment.

'I thought you were going to have a word with the cook.'

Bella was impervious. 'I did. The guys will tell you when she's ready to serve dinner.'

Lynda gave up. There were more guests arriving and she knew she would not part the girls until they had caught up on each other's news. 'We'll have a good talk later,' she told

Annis. Leaving, she added, belatedly conscientious, 'You're looking wonderful, darling.'

Both Isabella and Annis stared after her, speechless.

'Why does she always sound surprised when she says that?' said Annis eventually.

Bella giggled. 'Because she didn't stand over you and choose every single thing you've got on,' she said. 'She does it to me too.'

Annis's eyebrows flew up. She had her father's eyebrows, heavy and expressive. Like her height and her aquiline nose they were less than feminine, but Annis had learned to use them to good advantage to make her point. As she did now.

Bella snorted with laughter. 'When Mother saw me tonight, she said didn't I think I would get cold in this?'

And she gave an illustrative twirl. Across the room Konstantin was arrested. Not, thought Annis, by a tall brunette still wearing her business suit, no matter how much Alessandra van Herzberg silk scarf she had draped across it. It did not augur well for Lynda's cosy schemes. *Good.*

'And will you?'

'In here? *Darling.*' Bella rolled her eyes naughtily. 'Quite apart from the central heating and the fire, can't you feel all that hot breath in the air?'

Konstantin had stopped even pretending to listen to the florid man.

'Oh I can,' Annis agreed dryly.

'Anyway, I'm not sure but I think I may—I just *may*—be getting my love to keep me warm.'

He was measuring the distance between them. He was, Annis thought, going to come over. She was aware of a little flutter under the breastbone. She knew exactly what it was: the plain girl bracing herself for yet another encounter with a man who was going to look straight through her.

Well, that was all right, wasn't it? She hadn't liked it when he did *not* look straight through her, propping himself against the wall and laughing at her. No, of course she hadn't liked it, Annis answered herself. That didn't mean that she wanted to be reminded that no man would see her beside beautiful Bella.

With an effort she brought her attention back to her step-sister.

'Lucky you,' she said sincerely.

'Well, it's early days, but—' And Bella crossed her fingers for luck.

'You'll be fine.'

And she would. Bella skipped from love affair to love affair, delightful, delighted and ultimately uninvolved. Annis, who took a long time to get into a love affair and even longer to get out, could only admire her. Bella launched into each one with total passion. Then, when the passion ran out, she de-tached herself with skill and kindness and, as far as Annis could see, no injuries at all, not even to the male ego.

But for once Bella was less than confident. 'I hope so.' She sucked her teeth, unusually grave. 'This one makes me jumpy.'

Annis stared. 'That doesn't sound like you.'

'I know. Oh, well, life is full of new experiences.' Bella dismissed her uneasiness with a shrug. 'Tell about you. Who is the man of the moment?'

'Would I be here without protection if there was a man of the moment?' Annis said dryly.

Against her will her eyes drifted towards Konstantin Vitale. The Look very much in evidence, he was assessing Bella with appreciation, as if she were a new car or some other toy for boys. It made Annis want to hit him.

Unaware, Bella said, 'You know if you got a feller for your-self Mother would lay off.'

Annis flung up a hand.

'OK. OK. You haven't got time for anything but the busi-ness. I believe you even if Mother doesn't.' Bella looked round. 'Who is her candidate for tonight, anyway?'

'I'm not certain,' said Annis evasively. She had no idea why she did not tell Bella the truth. Except that Konstantin Vitale was now staring unashamedly and Annis somehow did not want Bella to notice. 'Whoever I'm sitting next to at dinner, I suppose.'

Suddenly very like her mother, Bella looked naughty. 'Do you want me to distract him?'

Not the way he is looking at you now.

'I think I can handle it, thanks.'

'Well, you've had plenty of practice.'

Annis managed not to wince. Bella would not have understood. She knew that her mother's matchmaking annoyed Annis. She had no idea that it was really hurtful.

Annis was saved from her unhappy reflections by the announcement that dinner was served.

'Here we go,' said Bella under her breath. 'Don't bite his head off, whoever he is.'

The dining room was a picture. The table had been extended to its entire length and covered with a starched and snowy cloth. Around the walls Lynda had filled every alcove and corner table with golden autumn flowers. Polished wood, crystal goblets, gold leaf and silver gleamed in the candlelight.

There were place cards but Lynda stood at the head of the table, skillfully breaking up conversations and directing people to their seats anyway. She waved Bella down the table to sit between two grey-haired men currently deep in debate. It underlined the point that Lynda did not need to do any matchmaking for Bella.

Annis looked down the table. Her heart sank. Yes, there he was. One or two of the men at this evening's party were positively devastating but there was only one lion in the jungle tonight and she had already met him.

He was standing behind a chair next to an empty place. The confidence blazed out of him. Oh, yes, he was much more than a peacock. The sheer physical vitality of the man was almost shocking. Annis felt her mouth dry, unexpectedly.

As if he felt her looking at him, he glanced up. Their eyes met. His were coldly amused. While she—

Annis drew a sharp breath.

From a distance he looked even tougher than he had close

up. Tough and sexy by anyone's standards, let alone those of a quiet twenty-nine-year-old with more expertise in business than men. And, of course, that was the place that Lynda waved her into.

'We meet again.'

'Yes,' said Annis gloomily. Her heart was pattering irregularly and she had the unpleasant feeling that her head was about to detach from her body.

She turned to look at her other neighbour. He was a tall blond hunk she had seen holding three wide-eyed women enthralled by his conversation before dinner. His hair gleamed as gold as the border on Lynda's best porcelain.

'Hello,' he said, smiling broadly as if she should know him already.

'I'm Annis—'

'Hi, Annis, great to meet you,' he said before his attention was claimed jealously by one of the admiring ladies who still gathered about him. In fact they stubbornly resisted Lynda's increasingly imperious hand signals to take their own seats.

'Great,' muttered Annis.

She squinted at his name card but it was turned at just the wrong angle. Had she met him before? He did seem faintly familiar, now she came to think about it.

Her mind scampered. Son of one of her father's friends? Employee of Carew's? Former acquaintance from children's parties? Sailing club?

In her ear, a dry voice said, 'Alexander de Witt. He was on the radio on Wednesday, television yesterday and will be all over the Sunday newspapers this weekend. You must be the only person in the room who doesn't recognise him.'

Annis jumped and turned. She met The Look full on. It had an intensity that made her blink. For a moment, everything went out of her head except how extraordinarily close the man was. How easy it would be to touch his face...to lean forward and bury her face in that brocade jacket...even kiss. Or be kissed.

That shook her. She said, more sharply than she intended, 'I haven't got time to listen to chat programmes.'

Konstantin Vitale surveyed her. For a moment Annis had a horrible feeling that he could read her mind. She set her teeth and tried to wipe out all treacherous thoughts of warm bodies and mouths too close. She braced herself.

But then he nodded, as if she had said exactly what he had expected her to say. Not a mind reader, then. Well, not this time. Her breath came out in a whoosh of relief.

'How long have you been a workaholic, Annis Carew?'

She glanced briefly at her father, at the head of the table. He was looking restless. Wives sitting next to him, rather than businesswomen, deduced Annis fondly.

'It's in the genes,' she said.

Konstantin Vitale followed her eyes.

'Ah, yes, of course. The phenomenal Tony Carew.'

There was something in his voice that made Annis uneasy. According to Lynda, it was her father who had insisted on inviting him, after all.

'Don't you like him?' she demanded.

'We have our disagreements.'

Not many people disagreed with her father and stayed on his payroll.

'What about?' asked Annis, intrigued enough to forget her uneasiness.

'Lots of things. Buildings. My timekeeping. Rights and obligations of ownership.'

'Good grief.' She looked at him with genuine respect. 'You've been lecturing my father on his obligations?'

He shrugged. 'I don't believe in ownership.'

'Don't believe—' Annis choked. Tony Carew was a master capitalist with very pronounced views on what was his.

'The moment you own something you want to put it in a box and stop anyone else enjoying it. That's a miserable way of living.'

Annis swallowed. 'And you've told my father as much?'

He laughed suddenly. 'Sure. He wasn't very receptive. But

I said to him, "Look, there are some things you may be able to lock up and keep for yourself but major buildings aren't among them. Too many people use them. Too many people *see* them, for God's sake.'''

Annis gave a choke of startled amusement. 'He must have had apoplexy.'

That gave him pause. 'You are very—frank,' he said slowly.

'I'm my father's daughter.'

Their eyes met. For a moment his were not unreadable. She had disconcerted him, thought Annis. And he did not like it.

Yes, she thought exultantly.

And then the mask was in place again and he was laughing gently.

'You are indeed. Well, you'll have to forgive me if I don't have the Carew—er—frankness.'

'You mean rudeness,' said Annis, interpreting without difficulty.

'You both certainly make yourselves understood.'

'Do we?'

'Clear as crystal,' he said dryly, as if he could read her like a book.

It was an unsettling thought. And she was even more unsettled when he said in quite a different voice, 'Though you're more of chameleon than your dad.'

'What?'

'I like the transformation. Turquoise suits you.'

He did not actually touch her breast where the evening-sky silk was draped. But Annis recoiled as if he had put his hands on her. The green eyes lifted, intrigued. She saw the sudden speculation there and could have kicked herself.

To hide it, she said, 'Don't be deceived. The plumes are borrowed.'

'I wasn't deceived,' he said softly.

Damn!

She said hastily, 'What exactly do you do for my father? I know you work for him but are you on the payroll of Carew Electronics?'

'In a way.'

'That means you don't want to tell me,' Annis said wisely. 'Why not?'

He shrugged. 'Business confidentiality,' he said vaguely.

Annis smiled. 'My father is in the process of poaching you,' she deduced.

'No. I'm my own boss. And going to stay that way. Though I guess Carew does a lot of poaching where he can.'

'Doesn't every businessman?'

He looked at her curiously. 'You tell me. Isn't that the sort of thing you advise on? Where to poach key staff?'

Annis laughed. 'If you don't already know that, then your business is way beyond the help of a management consultant.'

She thought he would laugh. But he did not. Instead there was an unnerving silence while he watched her.

At last he said slowly, 'You really are your father's daughter, aren't you?'

Annis tensed. She could feel the frown coming and fought it. 'Am I supposed to apologise for that?'

'No. No of course not. It's just—'

But Lynda had got everyone seated at last and the waiter was beginning to take the first course round the table. Annis helped herself to cheese soufflé and Konstantin Vitale's attention was claimed by the woman on his other side. Annis felt reprieved. By contrast, the massive but uncomplicated ego of Alex de Witt was a piece of cake.

'So who's here, then?' he said, smiling across the table at one of his admirers.

Annis hid her amusement. 'The usual mix. Carew Electronics. My stepmother's charity committees. A couple of neighbours.'

Alex de Witt was not very interested in neighbours.

'Have you seen *Totality* yet?'

And then she slotted him into place. He was starring in a new play which had hit the headlines. She almost snapped her fingers as she realised.

'No, I haven't managed to get there yet but it's on my list.'

A thought occurred to her. 'Come to think of it, why aren't you on stage tonight?'

He beamed. 'We're transferring to the West End. Opening next Thursday. Provided the director can get his act together, of course.'

Annis recognised a cue when she heard it. She took it effortlessly.

'Do you have to rehearse all over again when you transfer from one theatre to another?'

The actor's monologue carried them through the first course, second helpings, the removal of plates, a change of wine and the appearance of new china for the second course. Waiters arrived with large serving dishes of *boeuf en croûte* and Annis sighed. She had been well brought up. She knew you talked to the neighbour on your right for the first course, left for the second. Her respite was over.

Mentally girding herself, she turned back to Konstantin Vitale and pinned on a social smile.

'Have you been in London long?'

He did not answer that directly. 'Very smooth.'

Annis could feel her social smile stiffening. 'What?'

'Only it won't work, you know.'

Annis's smile felt like a rictus on her stiff mouth. 'What do you mean?' she said in a voice that was not social at all.

'If we're going to talk at all, tell me something I don't know. Like what your sort of management consultant does. And what turned you into a workaholic. Don't bother asking me pretty questions about myself because I don't play that game. It bores me.'

Her skeleton smile disintegrated abruptly.

'Well, we mustn't have that, must we?' said Annis furiously.

'I'll trade. One secret—that's all, just one—for everything you want to know about me.'

'I don't want to know a thing—' Annis began with heat, until she saw the mocking glint in his eyes. Oh, how quickly she had risen to his baiting! She drew a long, careful breath and said, 'Anyway, I don't have secrets.'

She did not sound encouraging. She did not mean to. Konstantin Vitale's eyes narrowed appreciatively.

'Yes, you do.'

'What?'

'Mystery lady,' he said, so softly that only she could hear.

'I am not a mystery,' she said between her teeth. 'And if you are trying to flirt with me, you can just stop right now.'

He did not say anything, waiting.

'I don't play that game,' she quoted back at him, goaded.

He raised his eyebrows, acknowledging a hit. Annis nodded coolly, half in triumph, half in simple relief.

Kosta Vitale looked at his companion thoughtfully. He really had been drawn to her the moment he saw her across the room. More than that, he had felt a shock. It was as if he had been waiting for her, or as if she was someone he'd recognised from a long distant, idyllic past. In fact, he had looked twice to make sure that he did not know her. But he knew he had never met Tony Carew's daughter.

And then, as soon as Tony had introduced them, Kosta had known this was going to be a whole new experience.

Annis Carew was not the sort of woman who usually attracted him. For one thing, from that first handshake, she had turned him into an opponent. For another, though she duelled well, she seemed to wince away from ripostes that she had asked for. He did not like women like that. They handed it out, but any man they went to war with was expected to pull his punches. Maybe it came from being a millionaire's daughter.

And yet... And yet... Her eyes were full of mysteries. Kosta was shocked to find how much he wanted to explore those mysteries. But he did. Through and through. From the height to their depths.

I'll have to be careful with this, thought Kosta, shaken.

'All right,' he said after a moment. 'No secrets,' adding

silently, *Yet.* 'Tell me about your career. Unless that's on the classified list too.'

She bit back a nasty remark and said with icy civility, 'I trained as a management consultant with Baker Consulting. I set up a partnership with a colleague six months ago.'

'That's why you're a workaholic?'

Suddenly she smiled with real amusement. It turned her eyes gold, like the lamplight. Kosta watched, fascinated.

'No, I've always been a workaholic.' She drew a deep breath and the gold died out of her eyes. 'Now can we talk about something that interests *me*?'

Raise your foil, Kosta, off we go in the next bout, he thought dryly.

But there was something he wanted to know first. No, not wanted. *Needed* to know.

'So who is this partner? The reason you don't date?'

Annis put a lid on her annoyance and registered a private resolution to rock the damned man off his complacent axis if it was the last thing she did.

In pursuit of this end, she sat back in her chair and sighed elaborately.

'I don't date because I don't want to,' she drawled. 'To use your own words, it bores me.'

It was not true. But Annis was in too much of a temper to remember that. Especially as she seemed to score a hit. Not the bull's-eye maybe. But a definite hit. The steady green eyes even blinked for a second.

'Dating *bores* you?'

He sounded outraged, thought Annis, pleased.

'I'm not keen on competitive games,' she explained sweetly.

'*Competitive?*' He sounded disbelieving. 'You must have dated some real oddballs.'

She flinched. *He's telling me I'm so weird no normal man would take me out.* It hurt. Of course, she knew it wouldn't have hurt if it had not been exactly what she was already afraid of. Annis felt her temper fly straight through the top of her head.

But she was too used to controlling her feelings to allow it to show. 'No, no. Standard issue,' she assured him affably.

His eyes flickered. 'They have my sympathy.'

Annis flinched inwardly. *That's what comes of mixing it with the sexiest man in the room,* she told herself, rejecting the hurt. *You started it. So have your fun. Just expect to pay for it.*

The woman on his other side said something. He inclined his head courteously for a moment, not taking his eyes off Annis. A smile began to lift one corner of his mouth. Not a nice smile.

'I don't think Ms Carew would agree with you. She's just told me she doesn't date. I don't imagine she flirts, either.' He leaned back so the two women could talk to each other.

That, thought Annis, was not playing fair. Theirs was supposed to be a private battle. He knew it as well as she did. But she set her teeth and prepared to meet him on this new ground. 'Flirt?' she echoed, smiling. 'Me? Why not?'

'You were the one who just told me to stop,' he reminded her, enjoying himself.

Her eyes glittered.

Before she could retaliate, however, Kosta was addressing the subject to the table at large. 'And I'm sure you're right. Flirting,' he announced 'takes Mediterranean flair. The English don't trust flirting any more than they trust garlic. Quite apart from the individual temperament.'

He glanced down at Annis quizzically.

He's mocking me. He wants everyone else to join in, she thought. Her heart twisted. She concentrated on her anger.

The other woman frowned him down. Annis had met her before. She was on one of Lynda's charity committees, a media personality. Now she was looking apologetic.

'I was just saying to Kosta that flirting is one of the great lost skills.'

Konstantin Vitale smiled straight into Annis's indignant eyes. 'And I told Sally that you wouldn't agree.'

Annis widened her eyes at him. 'Oh? Why? It seems pretty lost to me. No sign this evening that either you or I know how to flirt, is there?'

Sally drew in a startled breath. Konstantin Vitale ignored her. He sat bolt upright and stopped smiling.

'And no sign that you regret it for a moment,' he told Annis crisply. 'Like I said, no temperament for it.'

Sally murmured. 'Fifteen-all.'

Annis was hotly indignant. It felt great. 'You can't expect someone to flirt with you if you make her account for herself as if you're interviewing her for a job.'

Sally gave a soft laugh. 'Ta-da. She's got you there, Kosta.'

'What else is a man to ask her about when the first thing she tells him is that she lives for her work?'

'Thirty-all.' Sally was enjoying herself hugely.

'And when she tells him she's at the party to network.'

'Thirty-forty.'

Annis stared up at him. His eyes were curiously intent. She found she could not think of one thing to say.

'And that dating bores her.'

'Game, set and match,' crowed Sally.

He did not take his eyes off Annis. 'No,' he said softly. 'Not yet.'

And smiled.

Annis felt as if all her clothes had fallen off.

She did something she had not done since she was a child. She pushed her chair back with a harsh scraping noise and scrambled to her feet. 'Excuse me.'

She fled.

CHAPTER TWO

ANNIS took refuge in her old room.

There was an old sycamore whose leaves brushed her window, sending strange patterns across the moonlight. She would watch the shadow pictures from her bed. Now the late autumn branches were nearly bare. Annis shivered. They looked as exposed as she felt.

Why had she let Konstantin Vitale get to her like that?

She went to the window and leaned her hot forehead against the glass.

She could not remember ever feeling like this, so angry and muddled and helpless. Even when Jamie had decided that she did not add anything to his street cred she had not felt like this. She had just cleared all his belongings out of the flat and set about turning it back into her own exclusive island. Since then she had defended her home against the world and her heart against sexy, confident men. Defended them successfully, what was more.

So how had Konstantin Vitale managed to turn her defences upside down with a drawling quip that he probably hadn't even meant?

You're not a clumsy adolescent any more. You can handle any amount of drawling sophistication. So why have you let him throw you into a spin?

Annis put her fingers to her throbbing temples. The scar was rough under her left forefinger. She dropped her hands as if she had burned them. It was not often that she forgot the scar. Yet she had not given it one thought since she sat down next to him at the dinner table.

Well, at least her unaccustomed temper had done that for her, she thought wryly.

31

Come on, get a grip.

There was a small vanity unit in the corner. Annis splashed cold water on her face. She blinked at the shock of it but at least when she straightened she felt more normal.

'No more anger,' she said aloud.

She peered at herself in the well-lit mirror. Too well-lit. It showed the puckered skin from eyebrow to hairline as if a special effects' artist had just drawn it on. It looked as it had done when her mother had picked her up and had recoiled, her face a mask of revulsion. So long ago and yet Annis could still see it as clearly as if it was happening right in front of her eyes now.

Deliberately she put the thought away from her.

'Come on, Scarface,' she told herself wryly. 'You can hold it together. You've done it before. You'll never see Konstantin Vitale again after tonight. He's not worth wasting anger on. Just treat him as a short-term project.'

She patted her face dry and pulled the softly curling hair forward to hide the scar. Then, straightening her shoulders, she went back to face the music.

It was not as bad as she'd feared. At the end of the second course Lynda decided that she wanted to mix her guests around. So all the men were told to move six chairs to their left.

'I'll see you after the musical chairs,' Konstantin told Annis graciously.

'I'll look out for you.'

He looked at her sharply and she realised that the ambiguity was not lost on him. Sexy, arrogant *and* shrewd. Oh, Lynda had really excelled herself this evening.

But somehow the perfectly nice men who sat next to her during the cheese and dessert courses were insipid by contrast.

Crazy, thought Annis, applying herself hard to the finer points of widget design as described by her father's newest head of research. She greeted Lynda's discreet sign to the ladies to leave the table with relief.

They all congregated in Lynda's bedroom, fluffing up shining hair that did not need it and reapplying colour to make-up that already looked perfect.

And talking about the men left behind at the table. Of course.

'He's so *gorgeous*,' said Gillie Larsen.

'And tonight he's got Annis's name on him,' murmured Bella naughtily as she swished past with a box of tissues.

Annis frowned at her. 'Behave.'

Bella's eyes danced. 'You sat next to him and your heart didn't just melt?'

Annis thought of Konstantin Vitale: the Byronic looks; the intensity.

'Not my type,' she said with feeling.

Bella chuckled. 'Mother will cut her throat.'

'Tough,' said Annis hardily.

Bella delivered her burden and came back to sit beside Annis on the ottoman at the end of Lynda's impressive gilded bed.

'Seriously, Mother's going to despair. He was her *prize*. You have no idea how hard she had to work to get him here tonight.'

'But I thought Dad asked him?'

Bella pulled a face. 'You know Mother. Maybe she thought it sounded better coming from Dad. All I know is that she's been planning this for weeks. He's dropped out several times. That's why she wasn't going to ask you until the last moment.'

'Ah,' said Annis. So that explained the hurried invitation.

'And your heart didn't miss a beat? Not for a micro-second?'

She was not going to tell Bella that he had made her feel naked. Nor that her heart had been going like a steam hammer for longer than she could admit, even to herself.

So Annis put on her haughtiest business lady expression. 'What heart?'

Bella snorted. 'Don't give me that. You're as soft as Mother and me.'

'Not,' said Annis patiently, 'about alleged heart throbs.'

Bella shook her head. 'Don't believe you.'

'Look.'

Annis put her arm round her sister's waist and walked them both over to Lynda's full-length curlicued mirror. In spite of the scarf, her navy suit looked even more severe next to Bella's gleaming bare shoulders. Bella barely came up to her chin, fragile and restless and heartbreakingly pretty. Whereas I, thought Annis, look like a troll. A *tall* troll.

Bella put her head on one side.

'You look a bit pale,' she allowed, ignoring all the other differences between them.

Annis gave a crack of laughter. 'I did borrow some of Lynda's lip gloss, honest. But then I splashed some water on my face and it must have washed off.'

'When you ran away from the table, right?' Bella nodded. 'I noticed.' She swung round and narrowed her eyes at Annis. 'It didn't look as if it was anything to do with Alex. It looked as if Kosta had upset you.'

Annis said nothing.

'You shouldn't take any notice,' Bella said kindly. 'He gets so involved in an argument he can't let go. He doesn't mean to be unkind.'

Annis looked at her incredulously.

'Well, he means it at the time,' Bella admitted. 'But he forgets as soon as the argument is over.'

It sounded as if Konstantin Vitale was a more frequent visitor to the Carew household than Annis had realised. In which case, why had it taken Lynda the weeks that Bella had spoken about to get him to come to her dinner party?

Before Annis could demand an explanation, Bella went on buoyantly, 'And anyway, you made Alex laugh.'

'Bella,' said Annis goaded. 'I am a successful businesswoman and I like living alone.'

Why didn't it sound convincing? It was true. Only, in her stepmother's pretty bedroom, surrounded by designer cocktail gear and a heavy cloud of French perfume, it somehow lost that ring of truth.

And Bella, all smiling tolerance, made it ten times worse. She plainly did not believe a word. Annis could have screamed.

'I—am—not—looking—for—a—man,' she said loudly.

Gillie Larsen twinkled at her in the mirror.

'Go for it, girl.'

Gillie was a new neighbour and had become a friend in the last few months. Annis twinkled back gratefully. It also gave her an idea. She registered a resolve to get Gillie on her own when the boudoir crowd thinned out.

Meanwhile, Bella said. 'Look, you won't get near mother's dressing table for ages. Come to my room and I'll lend you some blusher, at least.'

Annis went. Bella cleared a space on her dressing table and provided her with a hand mirror and a palette of colours. For a few moments, she watched Annis critically, then took the little brushes out of her hands and began to dust in colour with swift skill.

Lynda put her head round the door. 'All right? Bella, the Larsens were asking about that guide to Ecuador.'

'It's in the study.' Bella put down the brushes. 'I'll get it.'

'Give it to Gillie, darling. She's gone down to the drawing room.'

Bella went. Annis picked up one of the discarded brushes and flicked shadow across her eyelid in experiment. She leaned forward to peer at her reflection. It was not impressive.

'Why does this stuff make Bella look like a million dollars and turn me into a clown?'

'Practice,' said Lynda, taking the palette away from her.

She handed her a small impregnated pad and Annis wiped the colour off her eyelid carefully.

'I could give you a session at Cosmic Works,' Lynda said tentatively. 'They teach you how to highlight your best features, what colours suit you best in various lights, that sort of thing.'

Annis dabbed away the last of the eye shadow. 'No time.'

Lynda sighed but did not demur. For all her apparent fluffiness, she seldom lost focus. 'So how did you like your dinner companion?'

Annis met her eyes in the mirror. There was a speaking silence.

'In another age you would be tried as witch you know,' she said at last.

Lynda smiled. 'A white witch, darling. You know I only want the best for you.'

And the trouble was she *did*. As a stepmother she had only one failing. While Jamie had been around it had been easy to keep her at bay, but since they'd broken up Lynda had been more determined than ever to find her stepdaughter a suitable partner for life. Annis was torn between affection and despair.

'If only your idea of what is best for a woman wasn't someone tall, dark and handsome to take all the decisions and keep her warm at night!'

Lynda laughed. 'Darling, you're so serious. I just want you to have some fun.'

'Well, I didn't have a lot of fun with this evening's candidate,' said Annis. 'He tried to grill me.' She swung round on the dressing stool. 'Why does he dislike Dad so much?'

'Does he?' Lynda sounded surprised.

'Not much doubt. And another thing,' said Annis, cheering up at the thought, 'he doesn't like me for the same reasons. Whatever they are.'

'Don't be silly, darling. You're always thinking people don't like you and it's not true.'

'No, I'm not. I just—'

'The trouble is that you work so hard you forget how to *talk* to people. Your father,' said Lynda in the tone of someone quoting the oracle, 'is very worried about it.'

Annis gave a choke of laughter.

Lynda glared. 'He *is*.'

Annis stood up. 'If he is, it's because you told him he had to be,' she said fondly. 'You know perfectly well the only thing Dad and I ever talk about is work.'

Lynda sighed and muttered. But she could not deny it.

Tony Carew might not have noticed when his only daughter stopped talking about James Gould and dropped ten pounds in a couple of weeks. But he knew the business plan of her new venture inside out and had a pretty good grasp of the partnership's current client list.

'No talking business tonight?' It was somewhere between a plea and an order.

'I've resisted so far,' Annis said kindly. 'But I thought you wanted me to network.'

'Not with your father.'

Annis laughed. 'OK. If Dad corners me I'll talk about Alex de Witt's new play. All right?'

Lynda beamed. 'Sometimes,' she said, 'you can be a lot less difficult than you like to pretend. I must go and pour coffee. Come down when you're ready.'

But Annis had a plan to carry through first. She cornered Gillie Larsen.

'I need a favour,' she muttered under her breath.

Gillie was perceptive. She detached herself from her conversation and moved into the hallway where they would not be overheard.

'What is it?'

'A lift home. I came by taxi and I don't want Lynda to organise someone into doing chauffeur duty.'

Gillie was not deceived, though she identified the wrong potential chauffeur. She grinned. 'Don't trust Alex de Witt's driving? OK, you can catch a ride with us. But we'll have to go soon. We've got a sitter.'

'The sooner the better,' said Annis with feeling.

'Poor Annis. Who'd have fairy stepmothers?' teased Gillie. 'Grab yourself a quick coffee and we'll go.'

Everyone had congregated in the drawing room. Lynda waved a hand towards the bookcase but Annis would have found the chair Lynda had designated for her with the ease of long experience. Far enough away from her father not to talk business. Not close enough to any of the artwork to break it, thought Annis, slipping into the low chair in the corner.

Someone gave her a tiny cup of coffee, fragile as glass.

'Thank you,' she said, concentrating.

Lynda had brought the cups from Japan and they were beautiful and unique.

'I said I'd find you,' purred a voice in her ear. It was a voice that she was coming to know.

Annis jumped so violently that the little cup hopped on its saucer. There was an ominous tinkling sound.

'Aagh,' she said, pardonably.

He caught an apostle spoon mid-air, one-handed. Then he took the rocking cup away from her.

'You're death to crockery, aren't you?' he said, amused.

'Not just crockery,' said Annis, betrayed into shameful truth by shock. 'I've been known to push my chair back into an Arabian urn in my time. The insurance paid up but it was touch and go. That's why Lynda sent me over here. Maximum shadows, minimum hazards.'

He laughed. 'Well, I appreciate the removal of hazards but I think the shadows are a shame.'

It was his caressing voice. In spite of herself Annis felt a faint heat rising in her cheeks. She swallowed, avoiding his eyes.

The delicate saucer was awash with coffee but he did not, Annis saw with irritation, spill a drop as he put it down on the bookshelf behind her head. He passed her a handkerchief.

'What's this for?'

She had to look up a long way. The little dress seat was very small and Konstantin Vitale was taller than she had allowed for. It hurt her neck and her pride about equally.

He smiled. 'You may want to blot your front. Or I'll do it if you like.'

Annis snatched the handkerchief and dabbed at the dark patch on the breast of her jacket. He laughed.

'Thank you,' she said glacially.

'My pleasure.' It sounded as if he meant it.

'Grr.'

A tall man whipped round at her growl. 'Oh, sorry, Annis,

did you want a chocolate?' It was Laszlo Larsen, Gillie's husband. He looked startled. He had probably never heard a woman growl before.

'No,' snapped Annis, still glaring at her tormentor.

Laszlo blinked. Konstantin took the gold box of dark chocolate truffles away from him and passed them on.

'Don't worry. She just likes things to be clear,' he told Laszlo reassuringly.

Annis froze. There was a horrible assumption of intimacy in the throw away remark. It was as if Konstantin Vitale knew her well enough to explain her feelings to third parties.

He sent her a quick look. 'Or so she tells me,' he added with an understanding smile.

That was worse. *He really can read my mind*, thought Annis, shaken. She was silenced, appalled at the implications of that.

Laszlo did not notice. He smiled. 'Vitale, isn't it?' He held out his hand. 'Larsen. I read your article on smart buildings. Impressive stuff.'

Suddenly she realised what he must be doing for her father. Tony Carew had a thing about smart buildings.

'You're an engineer?' she said abruptly.

'Architect.'

Larsen glanced down at her, surprised. '*The* architect. He's designed Tony's imperial palace on the river. Didn't you know?'

'Sorry,' Annis said, not sounding it. 'Lost the plot on that one. Too busy. I've been setting up my own business, you know.'

Laszlo, a banker, did know. All too soon he was telling Konstantin how brilliant she was, how her clients sang her praises. He went on until his hostess claimed his attention.

Annis drew a relieved breath and debated whether she dared risk picking up her coffee again. She looked at the high tide in the saucer and decided against it.

'Why am I so clumsy?' she asked the air.

'Why worry? It clearly doesn't affect your success.'

Annis turned her head. She wasn't flattered. Their private battle wasn't over yet. They both knew it. So she was deeply suspicious when he paid her a compliment.

'Success?'

'If you've got de la Court on the books, you're a success,' he said positively.

'You know him?'

'We have a lot in common. Small operation. High technology. Unique personal vision. Probably both geniuses, if he's on your books, maybe I could use you.'

'You could use a modesty transplant,' said Annis, outraged.

He was still pursuing his own line of thought. 'There seems to be a problem in the London office and I don't know what it is. Do you think you could handle it?'

Annis was tempted to say a number of things she would probably regret later. But Roy was teaching her caution.

'Depends,' she said not very graciously.

Konstantin looked amused. 'A good consultant's answer. No promises, no commitment.'

Annis curbed her irritation. 'I mean it depends on the problem.'

He raised a sceptical eyebrow.

'Look,' she said with heat, 'I've seen everything from geriatric product to a homicidal manager. I can make suggestions about new product lines. I've no cure for mania.'

'Oh, that wouldn't be a problem for us,' he said airily. 'There's no manager in the London office.'

Annis stared. 'You're joking, right?'

He looked faintly annoyed. 'Why should I be? Cut into the twenty-first century, Ms Carew. This is the digital age. We talk all round the world by tickling a mouse. Managers are an anachronism. Now, want to take us on?'

Well, that was probably the answer to his problem, Annis thought. Whether he would accept it, of course, was another matter. She had met self-willed geniuses before and they did not make rewarding clients. She pursed her lips.

'We've got a lot on at the moment...'

He did not moderate his triumph. 'I thought not.'

She narrowed her eyes and fixed him like a gimlet. 'But I can see that this one could be a challenge. I'll take a look and give you a quote.' She fished under the chair for her bag and pulled out her personal organiser. 'When would suit you?'

It was bravado, of course. She never thought for a moment he would take her up on it. Did she? Three days later Annis was still asking herself that.

Vitale and Partners had a small, crowded office in a late-eighteenth-century house in Mayfair. There were papers and magazines on every chair so there was nowhere for a visitor to sit. The phones rang all the time. The water dispenser was leaking and the coffee machine looked about to explode. People ran past her at the trot, shouting incomprehensible instructions to each other. The girl in charge of this chaos was standing in a half-open doorway being shouted at.

'Great,' muttered Annis.

She scooped a pile of glossy style magazines off the sofa and plonked them on the floor. That gave her somewhere to sit down. She did.

And rose swiftly. She had sat on an umbrella. It was nearly but not quite closed and a couple of its spikes had attached themselves like a hungry sea anemone to her smart grey skirt. It was also, she found as she tried to detach it, still wet.

'Excuse me,' she said to the girl who was still being rebuked.

The girl sent her a harassed look, turned back to the room from which the invective was pouring, hesitated...

Annis lowered her voice and, as she had been taught, *projected*.

'Excuse *me*.'

Everyone in the vestibule froze. Even the ringing telephones seemed to falter briefly.

Then another door banged back on its hinges.

'Workaholic Carew,' said Konstantin Vitale. He looked delighted. 'I wondered when you'd get here. You're late.'

'I've been here fourteen minutes,' Annis said precisely. 'And I've been bitten by an umbrella.' She gestured to her unwanted appendage. 'Can you unhook me, please?'

'Ah. I've heard about that habit of yours,' he said, weaving his way through the debris.

'Of *mine*?' Annis was nearly speechless.

'And seen it at work,' he went on. 'Death to household appliances and crockery, aren't you, Carew?'

He detached the thing and cast it back onto the sofa.

Annis retrieved it.

'You want an old umbrella?' he said, eyebrows raised.

'I think,' she said with restraint, 'that it might be a good idea to remove it before someone else sits on it.'

He pulled a face. Clearly the sort of detail that was way beyond his lofty consideration, thought Annis. She found she was shaking with temper.

He crooked a finger at the girl in the doorway. 'Lose this man-eating umbrella, will you, Tracy?'

Summoned by the big cheese, the girl did not hesitate any longer, Annis noticed. She also noticed that the girl looked at him almost with worship as she removed the umbrella from his disdainful fingers.

Annis took her first step as Konstantin Vitale's management consultant. It was pretty low-grade but at least she was asserting herself. '*No*. Don't lose it. Give it back to whoever brought it in. Make them put it somewhere safe or bin it.'

'Er—' said Tracy.

'Well, go on,' said Konstantin. 'It seems a bit micro but this is what the lady is being paid for. Give it to the owner.'

'It's yours,' blurted Tracy.

'Oh.' He stared for a moment, nonplussed. 'Oh yes, that's right.'

Annis repossessed it and handed it back to him. 'Somewhere safe. Or bin it,' she said again firmly.

He lost his smile. 'But I don't want it cluttering up my office.'

'Then bin,' commanded Annis, looking round.

Tracy gave a small giggle, hastily smothered.

'Oh, all right.' Konstantin snatched it from her and ushered her into his office. 'Great contribution,' he said ironically. 'Thanks a million.'

Today there was no sign of the peacock. He was wearing weathered jeans that looked as if he had climbed over a building site in them, which he probably had. His shirt was navy, a heavy-duty cotton and open at the neck. No concessions to the October weather, no concessions to the fact that he had a business meeting, Annis thought. Or maybe seeing her didn't count as a business meeting.

Annis worked hard at feeling affronted. It was better than noticing that his outdoor tan went as far down his chest as she could see. Or that the work clothes revealed muscles that she had only guessed at in the soft lights of her stepmother's drawing room.

Konstantin shut the door behind them. The noises of the outer office were muted but not extinguished.

Annis dragged her mind back to the issue in hand and sat down without waiting to be invited.

'I don't do time and motion,' she said calmly. 'That's just common sense. This place is appalling.'

'What?'

It was nice to disconcert him.

'Appalling,' she said firmly. 'There's no room, no method, no sound insulation. The filing is all over the floor and nobody seems to realise that for telephones to work you have to answer them.'

He stared. Too shocked to reply, she thought.

'I cannot *believe* that you run a serious business here.'

His mouth twitched suddenly. 'Haven't you heard of creative chaos?'

'No,' said Annis baldly. She looked at her watch. 'I'm wasting my time here. You don't need me. You need someone with a clipboard and a floor plan. And a lot of dustbin bags, probably.' She got up. 'Good day.'

He threw the umbrella away.

'Don't go. I do need you. Really.'

She narrowed her eyes at him. 'Why?'

He gave her a charming smile. It crinkled up the green eyes, making him look guileless. Annis did not trust him an inch.

'The business has grown without me really planning it. It needs some—refocusing.'

She looked at him in deep suspicion. 'Oh?'

He propped himself on the edge of a table littered with plans and drawings. He had not fastened his cuffs and they fell back to reveal muscular forearms. Her mouth dried. Annis whipped her gaze away fast.

Kosta caught the momentary flicker in her eyes. It surprised him. He had been beginning to think he was wrong, that there was nothing to this woman but her needle-sharp brain and a temper like an ice pick. That tell-tale shiver encouraged him.

But he was much too experienced to let it show.

'I never meant to be international,' he said ruefully. 'Even with e-mail and scanners, I sometimes think it's more nuisance than it's worth.'

He could see she was intrigued.

'Where is the main office?'

'Milan. That's where I started.'

'You're Italian?'

He liked her surprise. It meant that she had been thinking about him, in spite of all appearances to the contrary.

'I'm a mongrel.' Something prompted him to add, 'I set my own rules.'

Her eyes gave that little flicker again. He liked it. No, she was not as cool as she wanted him to think, businesslike Annis Carew.

'What sort of mongrel?'

'A wandering one.' To his surprise, he found himself giving her the full story. 'My mother came from a village on the coast in what is now Croatia. My father was on holiday from Italy when they met. She went to Australia when I was three.'

Annis looked puzzled. 'Australia? You don't sound Australian.'

'I took off round the world when I was fourteen,' he said, watching her. 'I've lived all over. I trained in Boston. But my first big job was in northern Italy. Milan is a great city and the Italians really care about their buildings. So I thought, why not stay?'

'It sounds like a real impulsive love affair,' said Annis dryly.

He gave a soft laugh. 'Oh, it is. Just like all my love affairs.'

She went very still. He thought, *There she goes again. The slightest hint of flirtation and she draws that breath as if she has run a splinter under her skin.*

He wanted her to stop doing that. He wanted her to flirt right back with him. He wanted to know why.

Instead she gave him a bright, false smile and did not meet his eyes.

'Surely every love affair is impulsive? I mean, it's not the sort of thing you draw up strategic plans and interview for, is it?'

It annoyed him into drawling, 'Oh, I don't know. You need an overall strategy, I think.'

She didn't like that, he could see.

'Really?'

She managed to look bored but something in the way she held herself made Kosta think suddenly, *She's embarrassed!* It intrigued him.

'Well, for instance, you need to know what you want.' He paused.

She said nothing.

'And what you can offer,' he went on, exploring.

Her jaw tightened. But she still said nothing.

Some demon prompted him to add, 'For example, with someone like me commitment is strictly provisional.'

Her reaction surprised him. He expected fireworks. He would have expected fireworks from any self-respecting independent woman and Annis was more independent that most. Instead she looked totally taken aback. Then—carefully—blank.

Well, there was no doubt about her independence. So what was missing? Self-respect?

As soon as the thought crossed his mind, Kosta knew he had made a discovery.

'You look like a woman who's just been told the truth by a man for the first time,' he said at random, trying to sort out this new idea.

Annis thought, *He's giving me a message. What is it? Surely he can't mean...Is he telling me not to fall in love with him?*

She pulled herself together. 'Not quite the first time,' she said with private irony. 'And I encourage you to go on telling me the truth if you want me.'

It was his turn to be taken aback. Annis saw it with pleasure.

She paused. It was her turn to give him a message. She added sweetly, 'I mean, if you want me to take this job, of course.'

One finely marked eyebrow rose. 'In spite of the advance publicity, are you flirting with me, Ms Carew?'

Annis refused to let him throw her. 'I thought you were the world expert on flirting. You should know,' she said with composure.

She opened her briefcase and pulled out a notebook.

'Now, I'll tell you what I'll do,' she said briskly. 'You talk me through the business. What it does, where the frustrations are.'

He did not make a sound. But she *knew* he was laughing. She looked up briefly, glaring.

'The *business* frustrations. Turnaround time on projects, staff, that sort of thing. Then I'll go away and write you a proposal. If you think we can help, you sign up and...' she pulled one of their new glossy brochures out of her briefcase and tossed it across to him '...we work on our usual terms. If not—no charge.'

'I can decide now,' said Konstantin softly.

The green eyes were bright with amusement. Annis refused to acknowledge that glinting awareness.

'Congratulations. I can't.' She settled back in the swirl of steel that Vitale and Partners favoured as an easy chair and prepared to take notes. 'Now, tell me—what drives your business? Individual projects or ongoing client relationships? How much do you pick and choose your contracts? And when do you decide…?'

Kosta answered her on autopilot. He felt stunned. So bright, so quick-witted, so clever—and so totally unaware! She did not even pick up the electricity that hummed between them. Or maybe she picked it up; she was just not going to let herself do anything about it.

He did not think she was a coward either. Which brought him back to that crippling lack of self-respect. It was amazing.

What she needed was an affair with a man who wouldn't let her take life too seriously. *I can handle that,* he thought.

She could get hurt, said an unfamiliar voice in his head. *This one's not your usual party girl.*

It gave him pause. But only for a moment. After all, he had set out his terms. Commitment was for the time being. Impulsive love affairs were for other people. He knew the road he wanted to be on and he did not get bounced off it.

Only—he already had, hadn't he? He never told people about his origins. He did not know what had made him tell Annis. Thankfully, she could not know how rare that was. But he knew. What if she probed more secrets?

He stopped right there. Probed more secrets? *His* secrets? His, cool-headed Kosta Vitale's, with his considered game plan and the achievements to prove it? Would Annis Carew be capable of upsetting that well-ordered strategy?

He thought about it while she went painstakingly through his business structure.

He reached a conclusion.

Nah!

It was not an easy decision.

Oh, she and Roy could help him all right; she was fairly sure of that. And he could afford them. She had been disconcerted to discover just how high an international reputation

Konstantin Vitale enjoyed in his chosen profession. She emerged from the articles in those glossy magazines with only one thought—how on earth were Carews affording him? She hoped her father was not letting his prestige, head-office project run away with him.

If it had been anyone but Konstantin Vitale she would not have hesitated to take the commission. But it was Konstantin Vitale. And she did not want to work with him for a minute, let alone several days of close consultation.

Why on earth had Lynda tried to throw them together? Annis could not imagine. He had nothing in common with her, that she could detect. Worst of all, he seemed hell bent on ruffling her feathers at every opportunity.

In the end she put her dilemma to Roy.

'What do you think?'

He was older than she was and he had been in the business all his working life. He considered.

'I think we could be making a niche for ourselves in small, high tech and clever. If de la Court signs up and then we get Vitale on board we'll have two of the biggest names in the sector.'

Annis fingered her scar absently. 'I was afraid you'd say that.'

'Don't you think you can do it?'

'It's not that…'

'Then let's go for it. We're too new to pass up something this good.'

She sighed.

'All right.'

Later she sat down at her workmanlike desk at home and wrote the proposal letter. Then she e-mailed it to Konstantin Vitale, feeling as if she had burned her boats.

The phone rang. It was Bella.

'Any chance of getting together? I really didn't manage to talk the other night.'

'Sure.' Annis was momentarily surprised. Then she remembered Bella's confidence in passing. She grinned. 'You're bringing the new man, right?'

'No.' Bella did not sound like herself. 'No, I'm not. I—I think I could do with some advice, actually Annis.'

'Advice? From *me*?'

They both knew why she was surprised. Bella had slid easily through adolescence without spots, scars or rebellion. As a result her relationships with the opposite sex had always been relaxed in the extreme. By contrast, Annis, who'd endured all three, found the whole business of sex and partners hopelessly complicated.

'I've got myself a real tricky one this time.' Bella was rueful. But there was something else there as well: something that sounded like real pain.

Annis winced in sympathy. But all she said was, 'Oh, well, tricky men are my speciality. But I can't tell you how to handle him.'

'You can tell me what not to do.'

'Ouch,' said Annis. 'Yes, I suppose I can do that. You want to learn by my mistakes?'

'You've made enough,' said Bella soberly. She was not gloating. Bella had held her hand through the last one, when James Gould had decided that Annis was too concentrated on something other than himself, and Annis knew how completely Bella was on her side.

'True enough. OK, I'll give you the benefit of my disaster counselling. Want to come over for a pasta?'

'You're a star.' It sounded as if Bella had a cold. Or she might have been suppressing tears. 'You sure you don't mind picking it over again? Doesn't it still hurt?'

'Only my pride,' said Annis, not entirely truthfully. 'No, I don't mind. It's good to remind myself why I'm not going to get caught in that trap again.'

And she was not.

It was more than pride, and she knew it. Jamie had stripped her to the bone. Oh, in her head she knew that he was shallow and self centred. Annis was very clear about that. But her heart said otherwise. Her heart told her that she was just not one of those women a man could love.

For six months she had poured affection into James Gould. She had even let him into her private sanctuary, her home. And he had left her without a second thought. Still what else had she expected? He had never said he loved her, never encouraged her to think that he might ever love her. Because, thought Annis, he had known at an instinctive level that he was an animal that attracted love and she wasn't.

So she would live without love. Well, that sort of love. There were lots of compensations—her work, her independence, emotional security once she was off that roller-coaster ride of sex and anxiety.

Bella would not buy that solution, of course, but Annis thanked God that now she was free from that cruellest of fairground thrills. Only for some reason, as she put the phone down, the image of Konstantin Vitale danced in front of her eyes. It was mocking.

CHAPTER THREE

'THIS,' Annis told herself aloud, 'has got to stop.'

She got up and moved restlessly round the room, fingering her scar. Even Jamie, at his worst, had not danced in front of her inner eye laughing at her. Konstantin Vitale needed putting in his place.

A thought occurred to her. She went back to the computer and tapped into the Internet. She would find out what the worldwide web had to say about her new adversary.

It was an interesting journey. Twice her telephone, on muted tone while she was working, beeped. She was too absorbed to answer. There was a lot of stuff on the net about Konstantin, including a photograph of him shirtless, climbing some scaffolding with a hard hat on his springy hair and a hod of bricks over a muscular shoulder.

Annis watched the picture load with disbelief. As the definition increased she realised three things: it was a very fine photograph; his style of dress hid a physique that any Iron Age hunter-gatherer would have been proud of; and he brought her out in a cold sweat of lust.

'No!'

She scooted her chair away from the screen as if it had suddenly reached out ectoplasmic hands and grabbed her by the throat.

What was she thinking of? Lust? Her, Annis Carew, Brain Box and Icicle Woman? *Lust?*

Even Jamie, whom she had broken her heart over, had not managed to rouse her to lust. He'd known it too. When he'd left he had thrown it at her in their last cringe-making clash.

'And as for sex—you don't know what it's about.'

Annis had flinched but she did not say anything. She never

said anything when he was in one of his tempers. That was one of the things that drove him mad.

'I can't *fight* with you. You just curl up and go silent and wait for me to shut up. *Fight back, Annis.*'

But she did not know how. She shook her head.

'You never wanted me,' said Jamie, lashing himself to fury. 'You just fitted me round your career.'

'That's not true,' said Annis in the cold, precise voice that always took over when she thought she might cry.

'Yes, it is. When did you ever run into my arms in the street? When did you even *kiss* me, for God's sake?'

Annis was shocked. 'I did—'

'No,' said Jamie, throwing his CDs into his gym bag. 'I kissed you. Always.'

'I—'

'Face it. I made love to you. Anything going in the other direction was just you being polite.'

Annis felt almost more betrayed than she had by his weekend with the office receptionist. She could not find anything to say. Swallowing, she watched her world fracture and fall to dust.

Then, true to form, she opened the door for him and wished him a courteous goodbye.

'If you shake hands with me, I won't be responsible,' Jamie said dangerously.

Annis shook her head. 'Good luck,' she managed through the thick wedge of misery in her throat. Briefly her pride reasserted itself. 'And I'd like my key back, please.'

For a moment he looked startled. Then he dropped his bag, tore the key off his ring, and stampeded down the stairs without waiting for the elevator.

Annis folded her lips together, went back into her apartment and worked all through the night. She felt hurt and humiliated. Betrayed. But slowly she worked herself up into the anger that she knew was justified.

She and Jamie were a couple. Everyone knew they were a couple. What was he doing going away for the weekend with a girl from his office? And how dared he excuse himself by saying it was *her* fault? If she loved him, he had shouted at her, she would have known he was feeling trapped and frustrated. If she loved him, he would not have needed to turn to anyone else.

Two years later, Annis allowed herself to think about it and found to her surprise that she could do so without flinching. The trouble was, at the time, Annis had thought she'd loved him. Even now, she was not sure that what she had felt had been love. She had certainly trusted him. She had been faithful to what she'd thought they had promised each other.

Now, thinking about all the smouldering challenge that was Konstantin Vitale, she sucked her teeth. It occurred to her that she had never really been tempted to be anything other than faithful to Jamie. Now she wondered what would have happened if she had met someone like Konstantin then.

Not Konstantin himself, of course. He was too sharp and too unsettling. She averted her eyes from that picture. Her screen was shimmering which made the image pulse in a thoroughly unsettling manner. She shifted sharply onto the next screen.

Which in its way was equally illuminating.

His business got several pages. An archive of newspaper and magazine articles demonstrated that, as he'd said, the company had begun to attract serious international attention about two years ago. An article on prize winners of the year said it all.

The driving force at Vitale and Partners is thirty-six-year-old Konstantin Vitale. Eclectic influences from the new and old world are seen in their portfolio of work, reflecting Vitale's own background in Europe, upbringing in Australia and training in Boston, Massachusetts. If you want a building that would look at home on a Singapore waterfront or a New Hampshire hamlet, Vitales are the architects for you.

But don't think you'll get to call the shots. Vitale has

strong views on buildings—'monuments waiting to be co-
lonised' is his current phrase—and he doesn't take or-
ders. These days he can afford not to.

'Well no surprises there, then,' said Annis.

He did not take orders. Would he take advice?

The doorbell rang. It was Bella, still shaking the rain off
her boyish crop.

'That was quick,' said Annis, slightly surprised. 'Sorry, I'm
still on the computer. Come in and I'll log off.'

Bella gave her a quick kiss and shrugged out of her coat.
She was one of the few people who was welcome in Annis's
flat and she knew her way around. She found herself an energy
drink from the fridge while Annis dealt briskly at the keyboard.

'Surfing the net?' asked Bella, wandering back.

'Strictly for work.'

'Really? Why?'

'Checking up on a potential client.'

That appealed to Bella. 'Cuts out the bills from the indus-
trial spy, I suppose,' she said, amused. 'What did you find
out?'

'That he's probably a control freak who won't take our advice,' said Annis gloomily.

Her computer told her it was safe to turn it off. She did,
and swivelled round to face her stepsister. In spite of the
amusement, Bella's pretty face was pinched. Annis did not
think it was with cold.

'What is it, Bella Bug?'

Bella shook her shoulders. 'Oh, you know. Nothing and
everything. What are you going to do about this guy? Refuse
his money just because he won't do what you tell him?'

'There are times,' said Annis, 'when I wonder which one
of us is the high powered businesswoman.'

Bella laughed but she looked pleased.

'Well, are you?'

'I'd like to,' admitted Annis. 'But then I say to myself, "Get real.'' The truth is that about fifty per cent of our clients know what they ought to do but haven't got the guts to do it. So they want an outsider to validate it. The other fifty per cent—the ones who really need our input—fight every step of the way.'

'So this new guy is nothing special.'

Annis thought of Konstantin Vitale's strange green eyes and the muscles on that damned Internet picture. 'Oh, he's special all right,' she said with feeling.

Bella looked curious. 'He's got to you, hasn't he? I thought nobody got to you.'

Echoes of Jamie! Annis managed not to wince.

'It's because just at the moment Roy and I have got too much work. But it won't last, so we can't afford to turn any of it down. Don't listen to me. I can handle it.'

'Don't you mean, ''I can handle him''?' said Bella mischievously.

Annis gave a superstitious shiver. 'I can handle him,' she echoed stoutly. But her fingers were crossed behind her back.

Bella's smile died. 'I wish I could,' she said unexpectedly.

'What?'

'Oh, not clients and office work and stuff,' said Bella with feeling. 'You know that's not my bag. But—'

Her stepfather, if asked, said Bella had not yet settled on a career path. Her mother lived in daily expectation of Bella announcing her engagement without any clear idea of the prospective husband. In the meantime Bella earned her living by doing various jobs for friends. She had cooked, modelled, managed champagne tents at polo matches and run a mobile disco. She had a full life, no savings and a lot of fun.

Except that it did not sound, just at the moment, as if the fun was that great.

Annis looked at her narrowly. 'What's wrong, Bella?'

Her sister flopped down onto the Persian rug that had been Annis's present to herself out of her first pay cheque. She buried her nose in the glass. Annis saw she was shivering.

'Love,' she blurted at last.

Annis did not know what to say. She felt helpless. Bella always seemed to be in love. She said so.

Bella shook her head. 'I'm almost sure this is the big one.' She looked up and her chin was quivering. 'It's horrible.'

Annis sank down on the rug beside her and put her arms round her. Bella let out a great puff of air and began to cry.

Eventually she pulled herself together and straightened, sniffing.

'That's better. You're such a comfort, Brain Box. You're the only person who would just let me cry.'

Annis stretched her cramped legs and turned on the fire she had inherited when she'd bought the flat. The gas-fed flames were phoney but there were times when they were comforting. Bella turned to the fire and spread her hands gratefully.

'Anyone else would tell me what to do.'

'I don't know what to do,' said Annis getting up. 'Love is not *my* bag. I'm surprised you don't know yourself, though. I've always admired the way you run your—er—emotional life.'

Bella blinked and gave a watery laugh. 'Don't try to be tactful. You're telling me I'm a flirt.'

'Supposedly a great skill,' Annis reminded her. 'At Lynda's dinner party there was great approval of it. Konstantin Vitale said flirting took Mediterranean flair and the English didn't know how to do it. I was very tempted to point you out as an exception.'

Bella's expression darkened. There was an oddly constrained silence.

'You forget how to flirt when you're in love,' she muttered at last.

'Do you? I'll take your word for it.' Annis was filled with compunction at the signs of strain. Bella took life lightly as a rule. 'So how do you know this is the big one?'

Bella scrubbed the back of her hand across her eyes. 'He doesn't notice me.'

Annis blinked. 'So?'

'And I—notice him not noticing.'

Annis tried to make sense of this. 'I suppose people do

normally notice you,' she allowed slowly. 'Like Konstantin kept watching you at the party...'

Bella bounced to her feet. 'Oh, Annis, you don't understand anything.' She sounded almost frantic for a moment.

'So explain,' said Annis, startled.

Bella moved round the room agitatedly.

'He looks at me all right. If I wear something wild. If I do something crazy. I can make him look at me if I put my mind to it. But he doesn't *stay* looking at me. He laughs and then he—looks round for someone who he's really interested in.'

'Are you sure?'

'Oh, yes.' Bella sounded sad. 'He thinks I'm a party girl with a short attention span and no heart. He's not going to waste his time on me.'

'Well, surely you can show him he's got you wrong?'

'I thought so. I've never had trouble before. But this time... I don't know... I just can't—keep his attention. And everything I try seems to go wrong.'

Annis felt helpless. 'What have you tried?'

'Everything.'

Bella prowled along the bookcase, picking up books and putting them back without glancing at them. Putting them back in the wrong place, noticed Annis. She did not say so.

She went on, 'I've phoned him. Not phoned him. Gone out with another man under his nose. Turned up on his doorstep with a bottle of champagne—'

'What?'

Bella looked round, briefly arrested from her sabotaging of the bookshelves.

'Don't sound so shocked. This is a new millennium. Why should it always be men who go courting with the drink and the flowers? If you want something go for it.'

Annis reminded herself that this was the sort of enterprise that she had always admired in her sister. Even though it made her blood run cold, she had to give Bella full marks for confidence. 'And did he? Go for it, I mean?'

'No,' Bella admitted. 'He made me feel like a naughty

child.' She ran a finger along the edge of the book shelf. 'Of course he is a fair bit older than I am.'

'How much?'

'Fifteen, sixteen years,' said twenty-three-year-old Bella reluctantly.

'That's a big gap.'

'So what? No bigger than the gap is between men and women anyway. We've still managed to get it together over the years.'

Annis laughed. 'That's true,' she admitted. 'What are you going to do now?'

Bella shook her head. 'Haven't the faintest idea. Show him I'm all grown up, I suppose.'

'I shouldn't think he's in much doubt about that,' said Annis dryly. 'Not if you turned up with your hair in a braid and courting gifts in your hand.'

Bella gave a choke of startled laughter. 'You've got a point there.' And, with one of her lightning changes of mood, 'You're good for me, Brain Box. I feel better now.'

'Glad to be of service.'

'Why is your telephone blinking?'

Annis looked at it without interest. 'Voice-mail. I haven't been taking calls this afternoon.'

'Hadn't you better listen? It might be urgent.'

'All the more reason not to take it,' said Annis with feeling. 'I thought we might order in a pizza or something.'

'Great.' Bella was back on form. 'I'll choose. You take your messages.'

There were four. Three from Roy, warning her with increasing desperation that their biggest client to date was having second thoughts about the start date. The fourth was Alex de Witt.

'Who?' said Annis blankly.

'Mother will be pleased,' said Bella punching the numbers of her favourite take away service into her mobile phone.

'Why? Who is he?'

'Oh, pu-lease. I don't believe this.' Bella cast her eyes to the ceiling before turning a mock reproachful gaze on Annis.

'He was the Greek god sitting next to you at the dinner party. He's in that play that's just opening. Single word title.'

'*Totality*,' said Annis, his message suddenly making sense.

'Typical,' said Bella grinning. 'You were winding me up.'

'No, I—'

'*And* you remembered the name of his play, even though you never go to the theatre. That's why you're the brain box and I'm the dunce.'

Annis was wry. 'I don't need a memory. He's asking me to go to it.'

'You're going, of course.' It was not a question.

'We-ell…'

'Don't lose your nerve now. You have to go. Mother,' Bella added solemnly, 'will be ecstatic. A hit at last after all these years.' And before Annis could answer, she said into her own phone, 'Flying Pizza? Hi. I want to order an artichoke and garlic pizza please. Extra cheese…'

It flicked a phrase out of Annis's memory. The English don't trust flirting any more than they trust garlic…

Damn Konstantin Vitale. He had no right to be walking around in her head like this.

'I'll go to Alex de Witt's play,' said Annis between her teeth.

It was a nice evening with Bella. It made the next day bearable.

It started off well enough. Alexander de Witt was faintly bemused to be called at ten in the morning but flatteringly pleased that she could go to the play. Konstantin Vitale, on the other hand, responded to her e-mail with the message that she was expected in his office at eight. And when she got there—by eleven, as she had said, having already had two meetings with other clients—he was not flattering at all.

'You're late,' he barked.

'And you don't read your e-mail.'

He brushed that aside, urging her through a panelled door. 'Well, let's get going. I've arranged for you to talk to the boys first.'

'The boys?'

'The main design team.' He indicated the room with a wide gesture.

Three pairs of curious eyes looked up from computer screens and a sharply lit drawing board.

'Good morning,' said Annis with composure. She smiled.

She had a nice smile. You could feel the tension in the room relax. Konstantin did not seem to be pleased by their reaction.

'I'll introduce you to everyone else first,' he said, frowning blackly. He was even sexier when he frowned, Annis found to her fury. 'Then you can come back and grill them.'

He walked her through the long, sunny room at top speed. Then whisked her up elegant staircases and down windowless passageways, opening doors and flinging names at her before moving on.

'You can use my office,' he said at the end of a breathless six minutes. 'Ask them anything you want. I've told them nothing's sacred. The girl at Reception will get any paper files you want. Bill will give you a password and show you how to access the computer records. I'm taking you to dinner.'

He was gone, leaving a whirlwind of flying papers and an alluring tang of herbal cologne. Annis picked up the loose pages, breathing in his elusive scent.

'Damn,' said Annis with feeling.

And the day slid inexorably into chaos.

She took up reluctant residence in his office. Exquisite linen-fold panelling sprang back at the press of a button by the all-purpose receptionist and guru to reveal capacious cupboards. Annis looked at them with dislike.

'Mr Vitale's idea,' explained Tracy, the overworked guru.

'Does that mean he likes things phoney? Or he likes things hidden?'

Tracy blinked.

'It's all right,' said Annis, taking pity on her. 'You don't have to answer. I just happen to like my cupboards naked and unashamed.'

Whereas Konstantin Vitale, she was discovering, liked to disconcert—and the room, with its eighteenth-century panelling, rococo mirror and ultra-modern steel furniture, did. She hung up her coat, brought out her big diary and mobile telephone and started work.

By the time darkness fell she had a pretty good idea of what was wrong in the partnership. It would take some time to prove and more to make recommendations. But the problem was as plain as a pikestaff, she thought. Konstantin Vitale.

She looked at a random sample of unanswered post. Some of it was two weeks old and it was exactly what she would have expected. One town council, one ultra-rich rock star, two prestige companies. All telling the same story. They had met Konstantin at a seminar—or, in the rock star's case, a charity gala—explained their problem and he had kindly made a couple of suggestions. He had said he would put them in writing and give them an idea of his charges but nothing had yet arrived. They would be glad to know if he was still interested in tendering for the business. They all ended with the same dread phrase: before Christmas.

She switched off her computer and the desk lamp, and rubbed the back of her neck. In the reflected sodium light from the street her watch told her it was nearly eight. Tracy had gone home some time ago, leaving her with a list of instructions on how to set the alarm.

Well, at least Konstantin had thought better of his arrogant command to have dinner with him, thought Annis. She tried to feel relieved.

She packed her briefcase and put on her coat.

The door opened and in walked the arrogant command incarnate.

'What are you doing in the dark?'

Annis jumped so violently she dropped her briefcase. He picked it up and restored it to her. There was nothing in the least threatening in his manner but in the semi-dark he seemed as tall as a tree. Her heart started to pound.

He did not notice. 'Are you ready to eat?'

That was Konstantin enjoying himself by disconcerting her again. *So don't rise to it,* Annis told herself.

'No, I'm not,' she said crisply.

'Why not? You're obviously about to go home. Even you must eat.'

She shook her head. 'I told you this was an extra task for us. I can squeeze it in as long as I don't get side-tracked. I've got to take all this stuff home and collate it tonight. If I eat, it will be cheese on toast at my desk.'

'Don't you need to interview me?' he said in tones of surprise.

'Well, at some point, of course.'

'Tonight's your only chance. I'm off to New York tomorrow morning. Then I'll probably have to go to my pet project in Calabria. Don't know how long I'll be away.'

'Now he tells me!'

He strolled forward. His dark hair gleamed. He had changed out of his jeans into something dark, with a wide shimmery coat on top of it like an astronaut's cape. It was only after a second that Annis realised it had to be a rainproof. It must be raining outside.

He shook his dark head and raindrops sprayed her briefcase. Annis flinched but he laughed. Konstantin Vitale, it seemed, was energised by the cold and wet. Cold? It made her feel hot just to look at him...

Annis said in a strangled voice, 'It's not fair.'

She was not talking about his diary but fortunately that was how he chose to interpret it.

'By my standards, I'm being exceptionally co-operative,' he said frankly. 'Normally I just call in when I get to my destination.'

'I don't know why you need me,' Annis muttered. 'A child of ten could tell you what's wrong with this company.'

He ignored that. 'And I'm giving up my evening.'

'What about my evening?'

He was unmoved. 'You told me you were going to work anyway. And of course you'll bill me for it.'

'I will,' muttered Annis vengefully, giving in. 'Oh, I will.'

He took her to a small Greek restaurant, surprisingly unsmart. It was clearly a family business and, equally clearly, he was well-known there.

'What's wrong?' he said, as the waiter took their coats and seated them in a candle-lit corner. 'Don't worry if you're vegetarian. They do a very good vegetable stew.'

'I'm not vegetarian.'

'Good. Their lamb is the reason people come here.' He looked at her over the top of his menu and his mouth quirked. 'So what is it, then? Don't like Greek?'

'Greek's fine.' She looked round. 'This place is just a bit—' she hesitated '—unexpected.'

'Oh? Why? Wrong part of town? Too unfashionable?'

'Not for me,' said Annis unwisely.

His eyes gleamed. 'Aha. You think I'm a slave to fashion.' He seemed delighted.

'I've been reading your order book,' Annis pointed out dryly. 'I would have expected you to go where the beautiful people go.'

'Would you? That's interesting. Why?'

The waiter brought them little dishes of *mezes* and glasses of aromatic wine.

'You normally do,' said Annis, remembering the files she had just locked away in his desk. 'Charity galas. Country house parties.' She raised an amused eyebrow. 'Are you trying to deny it?'

'No. I'm wondering why don't you approve.' He sat back and regarded her from under lazy lids. 'I would have thought you were more at home at country house parties than I am.'

She was genuinely startled. 'Me? Why on earth?'

'Rich chick,' he said succinctly.

She had the sudden impression he did not like rich chicks. Put like that, neither did Annis. She found that she minded him thinking she was one.

'Well, you're wrong.'

'No, I'm not,' he said calmly. 'Daddy is one of the fifty richest men in the UK. And I've seen your pad.'

Annis froze. *'What?'*

'Well, I went there first tonight. I didn't expect you still to be at the office—*my* office—at eight o'clock. I had the doorman call up, but of course you weren't there.'

She relaxed. 'I see. You went to my building. I thought—'

'I'd talked my way in?' He shook his head but his eyes were keen. 'No. I've heard how difficult that is.'

'H-have you?'

'Yes.' He leaned forward, his eyes suddenly intent. 'I like that.'

Annis felt the whole room lurch.

'Wh-what?'

He said, as he had said before, 'Mystery lady.' It was very soft, only she could hear it, and it set every cell of her skin quivering.

Annis thought, *He's teasing. You can't take that sexy voice seriously. He's winding you up again.*

'You called me that before,' she said, trying for amusement and succeeding only in conveying deep uncertainty.

'And I was right. Wasn't I?'

He was far away, all the way across the white tablecloth. He had not even tried to touch her. But he was stroking her with his eyes. She shivered as if under a physical caress.

Maybe he isn't teasing. Help!

She swallowed. 'I think you're imagining it.'

'No, I'm not. You intrigue me.'

Annis felt as if she were walking down a road she ought to know but in such a fog that she was lost. All the signposts were there. She just didn't know what they said. She gave a little choke of despairing laughter.

'Do you? Why?'

'Stimulus.'

Now completely at sea, she stared.

He leaned forward. In the light of the stumpy candle his eyes glittered.

'You keep yourself hidden. To a man that's a real challenge.'

Annis gulped. Loudly. She tore her eyes away and groped her way back to normality.

'Not to the men I meet,' she said with irony. She took a defiant swig of her retsina.

He laughed softly. 'But then, I've said before, you have clearly dated some real oddballs.'

And he picked up his wine and toasted her silently.

Her whole body felt hot.

'Great,' muttered Annis, as much to herself as to him. 'That's all I need.'

'No,' he said. 'You need a great deal more than that. But it's a start.'

'I meant—' She broke off. She could see she was in the middle of quicksand and the more she struggled the deeper she was likely to sink. 'Never mind.'

Change the subject, her inner voice instructed. *Choose your own ground and keep to it.*

So she pinned a sweet smile on her stiff lips and said, 'Would you like a rundown on my findings?'

He accepted the rebuff gracefully. 'So soon? Do you jump to conclusions, Ms Carew?'

'I'm very perceptive,' said Annis firmly.

He didn't like that. 'And what do you perceive?' he said, a shade less gracefully.

Annis debated whether to be tactful. Her professional self said, *Don't go to war until you're certain of your ground*. Her instincts said, *Go for the jugular*.

'Too many staircases and not enough coffee cups?' he jibed.

Her instincts won.

'Too many tasks and not enough priorities,' she said crisply.

'A brilliant insight. You could say that of any expanding business.'

'No, you couldn't,' said Annis now in right royal rage. 'Only when the business in question is run by a control freak who also happens to be a magpie. Do you know what I mean by magpie, Konstantin? Someone who collects anything that crosses his path, whether he can use it or not. You.' She jabbed a finger at him accusingly.

He blinked. His mouth opened but Annis was not giving him a chance to reply. This had been building up all day.

'You just can't resist, can you? You'll do any project anyone asks you to. As long as it's difficult and nobody else knows how to sort it out.'

She stopped, breathing hard. There was a startled silence. *And here comes the volcano,* she thought.

'Are you criticising the way I run my business? Or telling me I don't stand a chance with you?'

His eyes were slits of green glass. No teasing now. She had really made him angry, she thought.

Volcano or no, Annis found she was enjoying herself. 'The business. That's what you're paying me for. The other goes without saying. It would be too unprofessional.'

Their eyes locked.

Konstantin looked at her broodingly. 'This could just have been a mistake.'

'Oh, I don't think so.' She gave him her best smile, the one she kept for photographers at her friends' weddings. 'You may not be willing to admit it yet but you'll see. Believe me, you need me.'

Konstantin was stunned. He stopped looking at her as if he was a tiger prowling round a prey that he knew was smaller and slower than he was. He sat bolt upright and his eyes went dark. Even an impartial observer would say he was shaken.

Right thought Annis, suddenly excited. Konstantin Vitale was beginning to realise that she was his equal. And she was going to give him a run for his money.

The meal was not, understandably, a wild success after that. The lamb fell meltingly off the bone and the wine's bouquet reminded her of hot summer nights in the Aegean. It made no difference. He was curt and she, after her initial vainglory, was on edge in case he decided to get his own back.

It was a relief when he paid the bill and helped her into a coat.

'I'll drive you back.'

'There's no need. I can easily get a cab.'

'I always see my dates home.'

'I'm not a date.'

He sent her an unsmiling look.

'If you tell me again that dating bores you, I shall take strong action,' he said in a level voice.

Annis subsided. It seemed wiser.

'Thank you,' she said in a small voice.

He left his car in the visitors' area and took her into the lobby of her building, impervious to hints that she was now safe, thank you.

In the end she was reduced to saying baldly, 'I'm not inviting you in.'

He had regained his equilibrium by then. He sent her a quizzical look.

'It would disappoint me if you did.'

'What? Why?' she asked unwisely.

'There has to be more to a challenge than that. There's no fun if you don't have to devise a smarter plot than just walking the girl home.' He summoned the lift. 'I'm still seeing you to your door.'

They went up to her floor in silence, Konstantin humming gently, Annis fulminating.

Not speaking, she marched to a door, turned with her back to it like a prisoner facing a firing squad and thrust out her hand like a bayonet.

Konstantin gave her a kindly smile, ignored the hand, and whipped her into his arms as if he had done it a thousand times before. He bent her back in an embrace that would have shaken her to the core if she hadn't been absolutely certain that he was teasing again. She looked straight past his shoulder and saw the ceiling.

'Thank you for a wonderful evening, Kosta,' he prompted.

'Let me up.' She was so off balance that she had to cling to his shoulders and it infuriated her. 'I'll never forgive...'

And then the ceiling disappeared and she found that it was possible to be kissed by a man who was laughing his head off. Kissed, what was more, into a positive storm of sensation. There might be no passion in it for Konstantin. He might be no more than piqued into a moment's curiosity. But for a sober twenty-nine-year-old who did not easily lose her cool, there was enough electricity in the kiss to light up several cities.

Even Jamie, when she had loved him and thought he'd loved her, had never made her internal reactor go critical with a simple kiss.

Horrified, Annis pushed Konstantin away with all her might. She hauled herself upright, with the assistance of a console table. It rocked and water splashed onto the French polish from an elegant flower arrangement. For once she did not even notice what her clumsiness had done.

She had lost a shoe. She found it and stabbed her foot into it as if it were a personal enemy. She was shivering helplessly inside.

'Touch me again,' she said between her teeth, to hide that seismic throb, 'I *resign*.'

She banged the door behind her.

Outside there was a crash followed by an ominous dripping noise. It sounded as if the console table had finally collapsed. Annis stopped, momentarily conscience stricken.

Then she hardened her heart. Konstantin Vitale had made her destabilise the thing in the first place. Konstantin Vitale could handle the fall-out.

She bolted the door loudly and slammed off to bed.

CHAPTER FOUR

THE musicians retreated into the sunlight. Annis felt her eyelids flicker and fought it. She did not want to leave the dream.

As dreams did, it let her do things that in real life were impossible. She was dancing with a masked stranger. He whispered in her ear and she shivered voluptuously at the things he was saying.

They were in a panelled room. Its inlaid floor gleamed. Its doors were flung back to reveal a sparkling lagoon beyond. Moreover she was dancing lightly, sinuously, following the stranger's every move as if they were ideal physical partners. She, Annis Carew, who danced like an elephant with two left feet! And of course, now she remembered that, she began to stumble... The masked man was suddenly a long way away...

Annis sighed and gave up the struggle. The fantasy evaporated. She opened her eyes and stared around the shadows.

She checked. Yes, she was in her bed—she knew the poles at each corner because she had painted them herself. She knew the shape of the room and its furniture, although it was all in the dark. But the sound... In her dream it had been lutes but now she was awake she realised it was not musical at all. It was the telephone.

'How the—?' said Annis, sitting up in annoyance.

Annis did not permit telephones in her bedroom. It was her special place, a haven she had constructed very carefully. No anxieties were allowed to intrude into its sybaritic ambience. And telephones, in her experience, only allowed the problems to get through.

Yet somehow, in her temper last night, she must have brought her mobile phone in with her, instead of leaving it on the desk as she normally did.

Muttering, she got out of bed and began to search. Whoever was calling her was not giving up. The ringing went on. In the end she tracked it to its source—her handbag, thrown squashily onto the carved bench under the window last night. Annis fumbled with it, growling, and put it to her ear.

'*What?*'

'Good morning, Kosta, thank you for a wonderful evening,' prompted her caller.

Annis nearly dropped the telephone. It was the voice of her masked dream partner.

'Hello?'

Annis pulled herself together. She looked at the window. She had not drawn the velvet curtains last night and she could see the sky clearly. It was black, apart from pinpoint lights flickering at the wing tip of an incoming jet plane.

'It's not morning yet,' she said evilly.

'Were you asleep?' he said.

She thought with indignation that he was not even pretending that his solicitude was genuine. The little undertone of laughter was one of the sexiest things she had ever heard.

Annis shivered and told herself that *no one* sounded sexy at six o'clock in the morning or whatever it was.

'I still am asleep,' she said firmly

It was not true. At this early hour the central heating had not yet clicked on. She was coming more and more awake with every chilly second. Annis shivered again.

He dropped his voice deliberately. It was just like the restaurant last night, intimate, sexy and utterly deceptive. 'Wish I was with you.'

'You are,' she said, before she had time to think.

And only realised the implications of that when he gave a soft laugh. Her nerves resonated to the husky sound. She could still *feel* last night's kiss. Not just the imprint of his mouth on hers, the whole earth tremor.

'One day,' he murmured. 'One day...'

The floor started to rock again.

'Stop it,' she said between her teeth, as much to herself as to him.

He heard, of course. 'Hey, you're awake,' he said in self-congratulatory tones.

As if, thought Annis, that was the sole reason that he had murmured that suggestive stuff down the telephone at her.

But she knew it wasn't. She might be thoroughly unsettled. She might not be a practised flirt like Isabella. But she knew when a man was enjoying himself.

She gritted her teeth and took control.

'Right. I'm awake and ready to take notes. What do you want?'

There was a crackling pause.

Then he said with an edge to his voice, 'I thought I'd reassure you.'

Reassure! Huh! He wanted to wind her up and Annis knew it only too well.

She did not say so. Instead she said sweetly, 'Reassure me about what?'

'That I'll be back in three days.'

'Back?'

And then she remembered. He was going to New York.

'But I thought you didn't know how long...'

'I've put a limit on my stay,' he said blandly. 'I've told them I'm out on Saturday. So you won't have to carry on without me for long.'

Annis forgot she had taken control. '*Carry on without you?*' she echoed, furious. 'You think that one kiss and I *need* you?'

'That wasn't quite—'

'Wake up, sunshine. It takes more than a kiss out of a tango lesson.'

There was another of those pauses.

'Tango lesson?' Kosta was outraged.

When she'd first answered the telephone she had sounded slurred and drowsy. He could almost see her, warm and rumpled among her pillows. The urge to tease her had been irresistible. He should have realised that she would fight back as soon as she was awake. She always fought back when he teased her.

Now he turned his shoulder, talking quietly into his mobile phone. In his secluded corner of the business class lounge he was almost private. 'What are you talking about, a tango lesson?'

'That performance last night.' Annis retorted. 'Five-star dramatics. But a *little* short on sincerity.'

Kosta was entertained. He saw that his flight had turned orange on the overhead monitor light, indicating that he should go to the embarkation gate. He ignored it.

'How do you make that out?'

'A man who meant it,' said Annis largely, 'would have waited for me to kiss him back.'

He gave a soft laugh. 'Are you saying you didn't?'

He heard her shocked intake of breath. It was extraordinarily potent. He could almost see her wide, unguarded eyes. Her mouth… His body responded to the image as if she were standing in front of him. He found himself wondering what she wore in bed.

Kosta shook himself. Six-thirty in the morning when he was on the point of putting the Atlantic between them was no time to get thoughts like these.

To suppress them, he said at random, 'We'll talk when I get back.'

'Not about kissing,' said Annis firmly.

Well, she meant it to be firm, he was sure. Kosta could hear the way her voice was jumping all over the place. He smiled tenderly. He must have really shaken her up last night. He found it gave him a real sense of achievement. He did not ask whether he had shaken himself too.

The monitor went red. Flight now boarding. Blast. He could not let her go now.

'No, I agree. Kissing is better put into practice than talked about,' he said, and waited pleasurably for her to explode.

But Annis was fully awake now. Her voice had lost its early-morning huskiness and she was thinking on her feet.

'But I only kiss oddballs,' she reminded him blandly.

He laughed aloud. 'I said you must have dated *some* odd-balls,' he corrected. 'Anyway, that's about to change.'

She did not rise to that. 'Did you ring me at six in the morning to discuss my dating habits?'

The red boarding message began to blink, indicating urgency. Kosta turned his back on it.

'I thought you might be embarrassed about the land slippage in your corridor last night. Just wanted to let you know you can forget it.'

'What?'

'You—er—*we* kicked over a big flower arrangement. I got the porters to deal with it.'

There was a pause while she digested it. Kosta listened to the silence with amused appreciation. Working from home, Annis would know the porters very well, he thought. They would always be taking in parcels for her or arranging courier services. They had found the flower vase disaster very funny. Annis was acute enough to realise that—and to foresee that she would have to run the gauntlet of that amusement every time she passed them.

'I hope it cost you an arm and a leg,' she said at last between her teeth.

'Worth every penny,' said Kosta wickedly. 'At least it means you won't forget me.'

'Not much chance of that.'

'I'm glad you recognise it.' And before she could answer, he said, 'I'm going to give you my private number in New York. Nobody has it at the office, so write it down.'

She did.

'But why give it to me?' she muttered through the pen top in her mouth.

'They can use e-mail. You may want to talk more urgently than that.'

'I won't,' she said positively.

Kosta gave a soft laugh. 'I thought you were going to be

professional about this? You can't let our chemistry get in the way of your doing a good job.'

She did that little indrawn breath trick again. He could hear her thinking, *Chemistry!* His body stirred. He could have groaned aloud.

'Go back to bed.'

'Thank you,' said Annis with heavy irony. 'I'll see you on Monday.'

'You'll see me before that.'

In her chill bedroom, Annis felt the heat snake down her spine. Was he doing it deliberately or was it all in her imagination?

She said, 'But I didn't think you were getting back until Saturday.'

There was another pause. *Chemistry,* she thought. Her legs were trembling with remembered lust.

Then he said, shocked, 'You mean you won't be available on Saturday? Surely you're not a five-days-a-week sort of person? I thought consultants had to be flexible.'

There was a musical bing-bong in the background followed by an amplified voice.

'I've got to go. They're calling me. See you soon.'

He cut the connection before Annis had time to answer.

Just as well, really. She had no idea what to say. Except that she had no intention of seeing him again. And that was clearly pointless. Until this job was done, she would have to see him, no matter how much she disliked him and the provocation he seemed to think he was entitled to hand out.

So the job had better be done *fast.*

Accordingly, she worked eighteen hours that day. The staff at Vitale's were surprisingly co-operative. They dropped what they were doing to talk to her, worked through lunch, brought her coffee, dropped into her office when struck with sudden inspiration and indicated that they were quite happy to stay as late as she wanted.

'Why are you so good to me?' said Annis, bemused. Middle

management was suspicious of management consultants in her experience.

'Kosta told us to be,' said the senior draughtsman simply.

One of the young architects was more revealing.

'The place is a shambles,' he said, leaning confidentially on a big photocopier. 'Kosta's fantastic, of course. And some of the commissions are amazing. But you're always screaming down the phone at someone to deliver something you need like yesterday.'

The architects thought it was the draughtsmen's fault. The draughtsmen thought it was the computer guys' who thought it was the assistants'. Absolutely nobody was blaming Konstantin Vitale. He was their guru.

Tracy explained. Even she thought the boss was fantastic, but she was at the end of the food chain and most of the problems ended up composting on her receptionist's desk.

'No one will do anything unless Kosta thinks of it first,' she told Annis. 'Even the roof—'

She took Annis to the attics of the old house. There were big damp patches on the walls.

'We're an architects' practice and we can't keep our own roof dry,' said Tracy bitterly.

Annis looked at it. 'Couldn't you get estimates?'

'Of course I could. One of the boys could go out there and see what's wrong and draw up the specs. But—'

But Kosta had not focused on it. So nobody else did either.

'What *does* Kosta focus on?' Annis said grimly. 'Show me the e-mails he sent and received last month.'

Tracy looked appalled. '*All* last month's e-mails?'

Annis knew then. But she still ploughed through the messages conscientiously. The exercise also told her a lot more about the way he ran his private life than she wanted to know.

'When does the man *stop*?' she exclaimed in exasperation on Friday afternoon.

Tracy had just brought her a double latte from the wonderful

American coffee shop on the corner. She grinned in sympathy. 'No one can keep up with him,' she said fondly.

Annis snorted. 'Sensible of them. It's a wonder to me how he ever gets anything done. Look at this.' She stabbed angrily at the computer screen. 'Breakfast at the Savoy with Arlandetti; planning meeting in the City; site consultation with Carews; lunch with Melissa; evidence to the Select Committee at the House of Commons; meeting blah, blah; another meeting. Private view with Melissa. Dinner with the International Association of blah. And that's just one day.' She gave a snort of real exasperation. 'When on earth does he *design* anything? That's what they pay him for, isn't it? Designing buildings?'

'He goes away,' said Tracy simply. 'He's got a place in Italy somewhere. He just takes off.'

'If he managed his time better he wouldn't need to,' muttered Annis. 'Who's Melissa?'

'Who?' Tracy peered at the screen. 'Oh, her. She was a lawyer, I think.'

'Was?'

Tracy grinned. 'Last month's e-mail,' she pointed out.

Annis blinked. 'You mean he dates a new woman every *month*? I don't believe it.'

Tracy looked uncomfortable.

'You don't have to answer that,' Annis said swiftly. 'I shouldn't have asked. Sorry.'

Tracy nodded, relieved and left. Annis spun her chair— Konstantin's chair—round and stared out of the window into the late autumn sun. Even the dirty windows could not hide the golden leaves of the tree in the street outside. Did he ever just stop and look at that tree? Annis wondered. Or was he always too busy setting up the next month's social calendar?

It was all there in the e-mails, she thought. The course of a doomed love affair recorded for any clerk who wanted to print it off. Melissa had tried to be discreet, but being pursued by Konstantin Vitale had clearly been a heady business.

When he'd first met her, she had been constantly mailing

him in delighted amazement. Flowers! A surprise trip to Paris. Phone calls at crazy times.

Annis had blushed when she'd read that. Fortunately she'd been alone.

He seemed to be single-minded. Whether he was chasing a contract or a woman. He threw everything into it; the e-mails flew. And as soon as his quarry gave in he could hardly be bothered to return their messages.

Annis doodled a mouse on her notepad.

Once they were nicely pliant, the clients got delegated to one of his assistants. Melissa—and presumably her predecessors—was left firing off increasingly bewildered messages into the ether. The only thing he didn't seem to lose interest in was the buildings themselves.

Annis concentrated on feathering in whiskers.

Did he always lose interest in his women?

Presumably the answer was yes. If even Tracy, who thought he was second cousin to God, admitted that the e-mails showed another month, another girlfriend.

Annis gave her mouse a Van Dyck beard and a haughty expression.

She had actually, and ever so casually, asked Tracy. 'Do they lose interest in him?'

Tracy had shaken her head. 'Kosta wouldn't mind.'

They'd looked at each other with deep understanding. They'd both known that what she'd meant was, Kosta wouldn't *care*. They'd both shivered.

Tracy had said, 'Sometimes, I feel really sorry for them, you know? He just stops calling and they don't know why.'

'I can imagine,' Annis had said.

And the trouble was she could.

Forewarned is fore armed, she thought, and went back to work.

By the time she crawled into bed on Friday night she had put another thirty hours on the clock. Her shoulders were stiff and she had had to keep narrowing her eyes to bring the computer screen into focus, but she was quietly pleased with herself.

She knew what was wrong with Vitale and Partners. What was more, so did half the staff. The half that weren't mesmerised by Konstantin Vitale. She was going to enjoy putting that into the report, thought Annis, polishing phrases in her head.

Her work schedule had got in the way of her personal life. There were lots of messages from friends and family. She had not replied to any of them for a week.

Her father was understanding to the point of positive approval when she didn't return messages immediately. Her friends, including, Bella were philosophical. But Lynda was put out and Alex de Witt, calling to arrange to meet after his play, downright irritated.

She dealt with them all on Saturday morning. Alex said he would leave a ticket for her at the box office and tell the stage door staff that she was coming round afterwards.

'Great,' said Annis, hiding a sinking heart at the thought of a long dinner with a hyped up actor who would regard midnight as the middle of the working day. 'I look forward to it.'

Lynda was a lot less amenable.

'I've been talking to Bella. What are you wearing?' Annis was startled. She looked down at herself. 'Sweat pants, tee shirt, trainers,' she said literally.

Lynda made an exasperated noise. 'I mean tonight.'

'Tonight?' Annis knotted her brow in thought. Tonight was several thousand words of report away. She had not begun to think about tonight yet. 'I don't know. Why?'

'For dinner with Alexander.'

'Oh,' said Annis, understanding at last. 'Operation Get Annis Out More.'

'Well?'

It was easier to answer than argue. 'I'm not sure. Black?' she suggested hazily.

Lynda snorted. 'Designer black dinner jacket, yes. Dull office black suit, no.'

'Oh, come on, Lynda. You know I don't have a designer dinner jacket in my wardrobe.'

'Then get one.'

'No time,' said Annis truthfully.

She made a note in the margin of the stuff she was reading and took a bite out of her breakfast toast and marmalade.

'You can be so awkward,' complained Lynda. 'Do you know how many dinner parties I had to give to get you and Alexander de Witt there at the same time?'

'Well, you like giving parties,' said Annis, unimpressed. And then she heard what Lynda had said. The toast fell out of her hand. 'Me and *Alex*?'

'I know you don't like matchmaking. But if I can't introduce people I like to each other, what's the point of having a dinner table?'

'You wanted me to go out with Alex de Witt?'

'I wanted you to have some fun,' corrected Lynda complacently.

'But I thought—'

I thought you were throwing Konstantin Vitale at me. I thought he knew it. I thought he had signed up to taking out the millionaire's daughter. That's why I stamped all over him that first night. Or tried to, telling him I didn't date as if I thought he was going to make a pass at me.

'Don't think. Just go. Only not to The Ivy in sweat pants and trainers. *Grubby* sweat pants,' said Lynda forcefully. 'Buy yourself a new outfit for once. Live a little.'

'If I have time,' promised Annis. She still felt winded.

And with that Lynda had to be content.

It took Annis an hour of power walking through the falling leaves in the park before she had restored her equilibrium enough to go back to the report.

What a fool he must have thought her at that dinner party! What a vain, arrogant fool! Why on earth had he bothered with her at all? All right, he needed her professional services, but Konstantin Vitale was not the sort of man to admit that he needed anything. And he certainly didn't know how badly managed his company was. Yet. So why had he called her in?

But she knew the answer to that, didn't she? If his early-morning call from the airport hadn't told her, those revealing e-mails would have done. *He's interested as long as his quarry isn't,* she thought.

And she had told him in no uncertain terms that she was not interested, hadn't she? Heaven help her, she had done exactly the reverse of what she should have done if she'd wanted to keep Konstantin Vitale at arm's length. She had presented him with an intriguing problem.

Annis went back to the flat and worked as if her life depended on it. She finished the first draft of the hard-hitting report about four o'clock. Outside, the light was already going. Annis sent the document to print and stood up, stretching.

She was pleased. Thinking of Konstantin's face when he read it had inspired her. The words had just rolled out across the screen in a torrent. She would collate the tables and workflow graph tomorrow but she knew that would hardly take any time at all.

So now on to the next problem, Annis thought. She could afford to take a self-indulgent hour to wash her hair and have a bath. Maybe even paint her nails. But Lynda was right—she did not have anything suitable to wear.

Annis grinned, taking an executive decision. She hated shopping and seldom went anywhere she had to look glamorous. So in the last few months she had adopted a survival strategy that would have horrified Lynda.

The Larsens lived three floors down from her flat. Gillie had the wardrobe of a successful businessman's wife. She and Annis were the same size.

Annis picked up the phone.

'Hi, Gillie. I'm on the scrounge. I've got to do an after theatre dinner with Alex de Witt and Lynda's worried I might let the side down.'

'Come on down,' said Gillie, entertained.

Annis shoved her key in the pocket of her sweat pants and galloped down the carpeted staircase. The Larsens' door stood open. Gillie was already standing in the sitting room with a couple of garments on hangers.

'I thought you'd be in a hurry,' she said in self-congratulatory tones. 'I thought the little black dress and a really exotic shawl. There's a pashmina and a Thai silk print. Take what you want.'

'Thanks,' said Annis, taking the clothes and making for the door again.

Gillie followed her. 'Alex de Witt? Lynda will be opening the champagne.'

Annis paused. She had forgotten Gillie had been at that dinner party. She pulled a face.

'So I realised today. I thought she'd set me up with someone else.'

Gillie was disbelieving. 'Really? Who else would you look at if the gorgeous Alex was around?'

'Oh, believe me, the other one is an alpha class woman magnet. Horribly intelligent, bags of charm, all the sex appeal in the world and a tongue like a laser.'

'Wow.' Gillie looked at her friend speculatively. 'So why are you going out with Alex de Witt?'

Annis shifted uncomfortably on the spot. She was not really sure of the answer.

'I'm not going to go out with him a *lot*,' she said defensively. 'Just a couple of dinners to get Lynda off my back.'

Gillie raised her eyebrows. 'And where does the laser tongued sex god go?' she said, amused.

Annis permitted herself a small smile. 'I give him a report that says he's the worst manager in the world. And I never see him again,' she said with satisfaction.

She pounded off up the stairs, leaving Gillie open-mouthed.

The little black dress had a designer label and the Thai-silk shawl had a cheerful rainbow dragon climbing all over it. Annis blinked a bit and then shrugged.

'What the heck. In for a penny in for a pound.'

She rang the porters. 'Can you order me a taxi? I want to go into the West End.'

'Sure.' It was the younger porter, the one she suspected of being a poet in his spare time. 'Any more trouble with the flower arrangement?' He did not sound very poetical. There was a distinct snigger in his voice.

'It's fine, thank you,' said Annis frostily.

Gillie had lent her a soft wool cape as well. Annis settled the collar and realised with a sigh that her hair needed cutting again. She clipped it back, pausing only to flick the concealing wave forward over her scar, settled the cape round her shoulders and went downstairs.

The porter had come out from behind his desk. He was looking out through the glass doors and shaking his head gloomily.

'No taxis for forty minutes. It's the rain. I'd go into Kensington High Street and flag one down but I've got to wait for old Mr Henderson to come back.'

Their fellow resident was wheelchair-bound and needed assistance to negotiate ramps. Annis pulled a face.

'It's going to be that sort of evening,' she said resignedly. 'Don't worry. I'll go and see if I can find one.'

She did, spurning the part-time poet's offer of an umbrella, on the grounds that she would leave it somewhere. Huddling Gillie's deep collar round her cold cheeks, she ran down the private road, cursing all stepmothers, theatre and social life in general.

A long grey car had stopped at the barrier entrance to the block. Annis hurried past it without interest. And then she heard the quiet hiss of a super-efficient mechanism and the rear window lowered.

'Going out?' said a voice she knew.

Just what she needed to make a grim evening disastrous.

Annis halted and turned back. She could feel the raindrops on her eyelids and was almost certain there was one on the end of her nose. She refrained from sniffing but it was an effort.

'If you want your report, you'll have to wait.'

Konstantin Vitale did not answer immediately. For a moment he just sat there in the back of his chauffeur-driven limousine, looking at her quizzically. It was The Look, the one he had worn the first night they met. It said he only had to lift his little finger and he could command the world. Including her.

Annis hated The Look. And the silence that went with it. It made her feel hunted. She stamped from foot to foot, trying to keep warm while she thought what to say.

The car door opened.

'It looks as if you could use a lift.'

'No, thank you. I'm going to the theatre. You don't want to go into all that traffic. I'll get a cab.'

'Not at this time of night on a wet Saturday, you won't,' he said unarguably. 'Get in. I'll take you there.'

Annis gave in. She slid into deeply upholstered cream leather. The door shut behind her with a solid thunk. She saw that there was a glass panel between passengers and driver. As she settled her cape and shook the drops off her fingers, Konstantin leaned forward and snapped the panel decisively shut.

Annis felt her mouth open and shut like a fish. She stared at him, her hand stuck mid-shake as if some robot designer had wired her nervous system and then pressed the 'off' switch. She felt oddly naked and yet at the same time completely incapable of movement.

Konstantin touched her cheek. It was so fleeting that she could hardly believe that he had done it. Yet the jolt went right through to her frozen nerve centre.

Shaken, Annis felt her whole body judder back into life. Her hand fell to her lap and her throat closed. She tried to swallow.

'Have you come straight from the airport?' she demanded in a high, unnatural voice.

'Of course.'

His eyes were green and piercing and much, *much* too close.

'And you thought you'd check up on my progress on the way home?' she said ironically.

'That's one way of putting it.'

Much too close. Annis could hold out no longer. She sniffed.

At once Konstantin pulled out his handkerchief and handed it across.

'Thank you,' she said with as much dignity as she could muster. She blew her nose.

'No problem. Now, which theatre?'

She told him. His eyebrows rose. But he did not comment, merely giving the instruction to the chauffeur on the intercom. Then he settled back in his corner and looked at her.

'You've got raindrops on your eyelashes,' he said. He sounded fascinated.

Annis blotted them quickly.

'Who are you going with?'

She blew her nose. 'I'm not. I mean, I'm seeing one of the actors afterwards.'

'Ah. A date.'

Annis did not know why she should suddenly feel hot. But she did. Hot and uneasy and out of her depth. She straightened her shoulders and looked him straight in the eye.

'So?' she said, defying him.

'I thought you didn't date.'

'I—er—'

He stretched lazily. 'In fact that's one of the first things you ever told me about yourself.'

'That's the *only* thing I've ever told you about myself,' she said sharply.

'You think so?'

His body might be lazy but his eyes were laser-sharp. Annis felt herself slipping further and further out of her depth. Now was obviously the time to explain her mistake that first evening. Explain and—though it went against the grain—apologise.

She tried a winning smile. 'I'm afraid that there was a small misunderstanding the first time we met.'

'I don't think so. You were very precise. Crystal-clear, in fact. "I'm twenty-nine years old, I live for my work and I don't date," you said.'

'I know I *said* that...'

'I was impressed. So few women will come out and tell you what they want up-front.'

Annis was beginning to realise that, underneath the mockery, Konstantin Vitale was very angry.

She said stiffly, 'I'm sorry if I was rude...'

'Do I take that to mean that you *do* date? Just not me?'

'Yes. No. I mean, I didn't want—' She was floundering and they both knew it. Annis drew a couple of steadying breaths. 'Look, Mr Vitale—'

'Oh, I think you can call me Kosta, now you've blown your nose on my handkerchief,' he said, with a soft, ferocious smile that left his eyes hard. 'Don't you think that's intimate enough? I'd say that was intimate.'

Annis swallowed. 'Like I said, I'm a workaholic. I'm not much of an expert on intimacy.'

It was not a very good joke. It fell flat.

He looked her up and down. The lazy glance was calculated provocation. 'You know, you're an odd mixture. Very contradictory.'

He clearly expected her to ask in what way. Annis folded her lips together, refusing to give him the satisfaction of feeding him the line. So he told her anyway.

'Your father said you were a hotshot consultant. I expected a confident businesswoman, sharp as a whip.'

'I am confident,' said Annis, startled by how much that stung.

'In some ways, perhaps. So what is it about me that makes you defensive?'

This was provocation with a vengeance.

'You do not,' said Annis, her jaw so stiff with fury she could hardly open her mouth, 'make me defensive.'

He shrugged.

'You *don't*.'

'You mean you would be like this with your date tonight? With…' he waved a hand distastefully '…what's-his-name de Witt.'

'How do you know who I'm—?' But a more dangerous question pushed its way forward. 'Like what?'

His eyes crinkled at the corners. 'Like a cat about to spring.'

Annis did not like that. She went very still.

When she did not say anything, he added musingly, 'Will you spring on Alexander de Witt, I wonder?'

Thereby proving that, in spite of his bland pretence, he knew Alex de Witt's name very well. She was unwise enough to point it out.

He whipped round on the seat to face her. He was, thought Annis, taken aback, really very close indeed. Surely he did not have to sit that close in a limousine of this size? Surely…

'*Alex*,' he echoed in disgust. 'You do date, just not me. Tell me, what has Alex de Witt got that I haven't?'

And he dragged her into his arms.

It was not like what Annis had been referring to in her mind all week as 'the tango kiss'. It was harsh and, she thought muzzily, nothing like as calculated. In fact, if she had been asked, she would have said that Konstantin Vitale had not intended to kiss her at all and was not at all pleased to find himself doing so. His breathing was uneven and his hands only just the civilised side of cruel.

Only, of course, no one was going to ask her. Which was just as well, as she was incapable of rational thought let alone speech. And if anyone found out about this she would just die. Though, just at the moment, she could not have said why.

Annis felt as if she had gone too near a fire. She was burning up and the fire did not know it. A small protest forced itself between her throbbing lips.

He let her go as abruptly as he had seized her. A small muscle worked in his jaw.

'Sorry,' he said curtly. 'Put it down to jet lag.'

Annis put a hand to her mouth. She could still feel him, *taste* him. She did not move.

He said, unsmiling, 'No need to look like that. You call a halt. I respect it. I don't force myself on women.'

Annis flushed horribly. 'I never thought...'

'Didn't you? Then it's a good imitation you've got there.'

He was more than angry. He was *furious*. What was more, even Annis was experienced enough to recognise that he was at least as angry with himself as he was with her.

She said shakily, 'Why are you like this? I don't understand.'

'Don't you?' It was his turn to draw a long breath. 'Then maybe you need chemistry lessons.' He was not smiling.

She made a helpless gesture.

'I'm sorry. It's like you said on the phone. I'm no good at chemistry.'

She tried to smile but it went badly awry.

He cupped her face and looked deep into her eyes. It was an odd gesture, awkward, reluctant even. 'Maybe we both need lessons.' His voice was curt.

The limousine was inching its way through the crowds. Some people bent to see who was in the long, powerful car. Annis suddenly realised any one of them could have spied on that fierce kiss. Certainly the driver would have had seen it in his mirror. Her whole body flinched at the thought.

She hauled the cape round her like a magic cloak.

He said, 'Annis, I—Don't look like that. I never meant—'

'I know. It was chemistry,' she said, suddenly savage. 'Out of your control and mine. The perfect excuse for any damned thing you want to do.'

He said gently, 'Not an excuse. A reason. A powerful reason.'

And he touched her face again, as if he could not help himself.

Annis shivered with that terrible longing she had never known before.

Whipping herself into saving anger, she flung at him, 'Chemistry! Garbage! What you need is a lesson in civilised behaviour.'

His hand fell.

The car edged along St Martin's Lane. Neon signs for plays, movies and bistros vied with a bewildering array of traffic lights on all sides and at every angle. Annis found that the brilliant outlines were blurring. She dashed an angry hand across her eyes.

'Rational people don't *do* things like that,' she said not very clearly.

Konstantin still said nothing. There was a strange, blank look in his eyes.

The traffic light turned red. The car glided to an expensive halt.

Why didn't he say something?

Annis could feel treacherous tears rising again. She could not understand it. She felt as if she were a teenager again full of uncertainty and rioting hormones.

'Oh, this is *crazy*,' she exploded.

She fumbled briefly with the handle and tumbled out among the traffic and the cheerful pedestrians weaving between the cars.

'Thank you for the lift,' she said, not meaning a word of it.

And slammed the door on his look of dawning alarm.

She dived for the theatre without a backward look.

CHAPTER FIVE

ANNIS hardly took in a word of the play. Her thoughts returned inexorably to Konstantin. How he had looked; what he had said. The shockingly uncontrolled kiss in the limousine. In the dark of the theatre she admitted to herself that it was not just Konstantin who had been uncontrolled.

What is happening to me? I am not like this.

She kept touching a hand to her lips as if she could brush away the imprint of his mouth. She did not manage it.

Dinner could have been a disaster. The image across the table from her kept dissolving from Alex de Witt's handsome features to a dark, furious face. And then, worse, that face turned to an appalled and silent blankness as he realised—what? Annis had to keep giving herself a mental shake and large gulps of iced water to bring her back to the here and now.

Fortunately the restaurant was full of people who were determined to claim Alex de Witt's attention away from her. They came up in a steady stream to congratulate him or to exchange telephone numbers. So many people, in fact, that he was more often slewed around in his chair, talking to someone else, than he was talking to her. There was a chance, thought Annis, that Alex did not even notice that she was only half with him.

He took her home in a taxi.

'I won't ask you in,' she said, as he saw her courteously into the building. 'I'm sure you must be exhausted. Such a powerful performance.'

Kosta would not have accepted it for a moment, she thought. But Alex de Witt saw nothing evasive there. Easily, he bent and kissed her goodnight. Then, with a casual wave, he was gone.

Annis was grateful for that kiss. It had been pleasurable, practised, and it had left absolutely no shadow pressure on her mouth afterwards. Nothing to keep her awake at night.

Back to normal, she told herself thankfully.

But she wasn't. Nothing was normal. She could not sleep, though she tried, and it had nothing to do with the glamorous Alexander de Witt.

'Damn,' said Annis, struggling up on one elbow after a useless battle with the images behind her closed eyelids.

She gave up and pushed the bedclothes back. Then she padded out to the kitchen and made herself a large and comforting pot of tea. She put some soothing piano music on the stereo.

It was no good. Under the Mozart, she could still hear a man's low voice saying savagely, 'Maybe you need chemistry lessons.'

Annis wrapped her arms round herself. She could not remember that anyone had ever made her feel so inadequate before. So *gauche.* As if she were not quite a woman. And yet at the same time reminded every atom in her body that she could not escape the imperatives of her womanhood.

'That is nonsense and you know it,' Annis told herself loudly.

But it wasn't. She could cope when Konstantin laughed at her. She could even cope with his equivocal teasing, although she was not as polished at repartee as Bella and at least once he had had her blush.

But, 'you need chemistry lessons'! That was what she could not cope with. There was no teasing in that. It was straightforward contempt. It sounded as if he despised her from the bottom of his heart. That thought left her feeling cold and vulnerable, and very, very small.

She cradled the mug of tea to her breast, trying to warm herself.

'Overreaction,' she said, trying to be sensible. 'What does

it matter, even if he does despise you? He's a client for
heaven's sake. He doesn't have to be in love with you.'

But I want—

She spilled her tea.

'No, you don't,' she said very loudly indeed.

And replaced Mozart with a pacey Brazilian samba com-
pilation that would have had the neighbours pounding on the
walls if the block had not been sound-proofed to a level that
would have muffled cannon-fire.

She worked through the night.

She fully expected Konstantin to turn up the next day. Or at
least to telephone. She told the porters to be *certain* to call up
when any visitor arrived for her, no matter how well they
thought they knew him. And she screened all her calls.

It was all quite pointless. Konstantin Vitale stayed resolutely
silent. Alex de Witt rang to allow her to thank him for dinner.
The mother of her godson asked her to the child's birthday
party. Roy rang, worrying about their big contract and sum-
moning her to a meeting first thing on Monday morning. She
answered them all distractedly and rang off as soon as she
could.

Lynda, finding Annis positively pliant in the matter of going
to a charity dance the following Saturday, was concerned.

'Are you all right?'

'I'm fine,' said Annis wearily.

It was eleven-thirty in the morning and she had been working for nearly eight hours.

'You did hear what I said?'

Annis peered at her telephone pad.

'Save the rainforest. Bash next Saturday, Godwin House.
Drinks with you and Dad at seven-thirty.'

'And you don't mind?'

Annis gave a ghostly chuckle. 'I wouldn't go that far. I just
said I'd be there.'

Lynda digested this.

'Do you—er—want to bring anyone?'

Annis could not help herself. Konstantin's harsh face flipped in front of her eyes.

'No.'

'No need to shout,' said Lynda, injured. 'Didn't the dinner with Alex go well, then?'

'Dinner…?' Oh, so that was what this call was about. 'Dinner with Alex was fine.'

'Because I'd be happy to ask him…'

Annis sought for an excuse and was inspired. 'Surely an actor in a new West End play would be working on a Saturday night?'

There was a frustrated silence.

'I hadn't thought of that,' admitted Lynda. 'Well, I'll think of someone.' She added unguardedly, 'I thought I'd got my table filled but the Larsens have dropped out.'

'Well, if you can find a matching pair, cross me off and you're even again,' said Annis, preparing to ring off.

'It's very formal,' Lynda said, raising her voice and speeding up. 'You will remember, won't you? I mean, you'll need something really dressy.'

It sounded like another assignment for style consultant Larsen, thought Annis. She did not say so.

'I'll break out the magic ball-dress and glass slippers,' she promised. She rang off before Lynda could demand more details.

She scribbled the entry in her diary and promptly forgot about it. The diary was very full between now and next Saturday. Anyway, after presenting Konstantin with her assassination of his management technique, she thought ruefully, maybe she would not even survive. To say nothing of the make-or-break meeting with the major client that Roy had arranged for Monday.

She went to bed early and slept no better. If Konstantin had been in the room with her she could not have been more conscious of him. Annis tried to convince herself that she was worried about what he would say when he read her report.

But it was not that and she knew it in her heart of hearts. It was that damned *chemistry.*

'The sooner I'm out of Vitale and Partners the better,' Annis told herself.

The next morning she had three copies of her report bound at the small jobbing printers she used and jumped into a taxi.

'I want to go to the City. But I need to drop something off in Mayfair first.'

The shops still had all their night-time illuminations on. The streets were empty of pedestrians, although traffic was building up in the main routes. But the taxi driver was relaxed when she asked him to pull into the kerb and wait outside Vitale's elegant Mayfair premises.

Without a light anywhere, the Adam house was pretty as an illustration from a Jane Austen novel. Annis used her key and incongruous security code to slip into the empty building. She switched on the light and the eighteenth-century illusion vanished. The reception area was untidy as always and remorselessly contemporary.

She hesitated. No, not a good idea to leave the report at the reception desk. It would only get lost in the general debris. She would put it on Konstantin's desk.

She opened the door to his office.

There was a pool of light from an angled lamp on his desk but his chair was empty. He must have come into work yesterday and forgotten to turn it off when he left, thought Annis. Her high heels pattered rapidly across the parquet flooring.

'Good morning,' said a husky voice behind her.

She skidded, spinning round. The top copy of her pile of reports flew into the air. Konstantin fielded it one-handed.

'Is that for me?'

He was in his shirtsleeves. The dark hair flopped wildly. *He's been running his hands through it all night,* thought Annis, taken aback. His eyes were creased up, as if he was too tired to focus properly, and his jaw was shadowed by at least a day's stubble. He had pushed up his shirtsleeves to reveal sinewy forearms. Above them his biceps were evident under the creased cotton.

So that's why he's so strong, thought Annis involuntarily.

She flushed and looked away. She did not want to think about how strong he was. Nor how she had found it out.

'Three copies,' she said, making a very respectable recovery. She'd be all right as long as she did not actually look at him. 'I suggest you let people have a look at it as soon as possible. They've spent a lot of time talking to me. You don't want them getting unnecessarily anxious.'

'Then why don't you talk to them about it?'

It was a reasonable enough suggestion but he sounded absent. No, that wasn't right. He sounded *constrained*.

Annis forgot that she was not supposed to be looking at him. His attitude was more than tiredness, more than preoccupation. He looked as if somewhere in the night a revelation had hit him. Not, if Annis was any judge, a welcome revelation. He looked as if he was coming back to normal slowly and groggily and her arrival had somehow stirred the pot again.

She met his eyes unguardedly. He went very still. The green eyes grew alert, then intent. Annis started to drown...

He said her name softly.

'I—' She did not know what she wanted to say. How could he look at her like that, as if he had never seen her before? 'Your staff—'

He cast the papers away from him and came towards her.

'Won't be in for hours.'

Annis heard herself say, 'You—you should take them through my report soon.' But his eyes were boring into hers and it was like speaking a foreign language.

He said softly, 'When everyone's arrived, I'll get them in here and you can do it yourself. In the meantime...'

Annis tore her eyes away. It hurt, like a physical pain.

I want him to touch me. I can't afford to let him touch me.

She took a step back and looked at her watch. 'No time. Sorry.'

He stopped abruptly. His eyes narrowed to slits.

'I see.'

Annis swallowed. She found a defensive note creeping into her voice. 'I'm due in the City for my next meeting.'

He took the other two reports from her and slammed them down on his desk without so much as glancing at them. Annis jumped.

'So you thought you'd slip them in here while the place was deserted.'

'No,' she said with dignity. 'I thought I—'

'Would avoid seeing me.' No melting softness now. The clipped voice was icy. He looked her up and down unflatteringly. 'I ask myself why.'

'You're talking nonsense.'

He ignored that. 'And I can only think of two reasons.' He numbered them on his long fingers. 'One: the report is so damn poor that you're ashamed of it.'

Annis forgot she was on the defensive. 'How dare you?'

He ignored that too. 'Or two: you're still running scared of the chemical reaction when we get together.'

'I am not,' said Annis between her teeth, 'scared of anything.'

He gave her a glittering, false smile. 'I think we both know that's not true. One taste of real life and you panic as if the barbarians have arrived.' The cold voice lashed at her.

Annis stared. What on earth had she done to make him this angry? He had not even read what she'd said about his management style yet. It couldn't be because she had just turned him down. It couldn't have been a serious approach. No one made passes in the office at the start of the working day. Especially not super sexy sophisticates like Konstantin Vitale. It was a tease, a mockery of flirtation, designed to wind up someone who did not know how to flirt.

Wasn't it?

All her instincts were buzzing deafeningly. Out of the chaos one explanation shouted at her. Unwisely Annis flung it at him.

'This is because I said you need a lesson in civilised behaviour, isn't it?'

For a moment the lines on his face deepened murderously. Then he turned away, stabbing a hand through his unruly hair. 'Of course not.'

Annis was trembling with reaction. *Ridiculous,* she told herself.

She told him in as reasonable a voice as she could manage, 'I stand by that. You were out of order on Saturday night.'

He did not reply.

Goaded by some demon—knowing even as the words came out that she should not be saying this, not now, not to him—she went on, 'And I didn't *panic.* I'm a grown woman. I don't panic just because some lout lays hands on me. I can—'

He swung round on her. She stopped as if she had walked into a wall.

There was such a blaze of anger in his eyes that Annis quailed. She could not help herself. She took an involuntary step back.

A mirthless smile twisted one corner of his mouth. 'Still not panicking, Ms Carew? I'm impressed.'

She felt winded. Cold. In uncharted territory without a compass.

'I never panic,' she said slowly. Her own feelings bewildered her.

It was true. She had always had steady nerves. She had made mistakes, overreached herself, made bad calls. But she had never panicked. Until now.

She stared at him, her eyes widening. It was slowly dawning on her that not just the situation but her own reaction was new, frighteningly new. She had never felt like this before and she did not know what to do about it.

The heat died out of his eyes. The silence lengthened. He turned away, shaking his head.

Annis gave herself a little shake. 'I have to go,' she said in a stunned voice.

With his back to her he said, 'I'll call you when I've read the report.'

'What?'

She focused on him. He was leaning on the desk, his head bent. The angled lamp caught his long-fingered hands in a cruel spotlight. They were white with tension.

She said loudly, not really knowing why, 'Maybe I'm not the only one who is panicking.'

His hands flinched.

'Maybe you're not.' It was so quiet it was almost inaudible. And, while she was wondering if she had heard what she thought she heard, Konstantin straightened and added in his crisp ordinary voice, 'Go to your meeting.'

She hesitated, bewildered.

He turned and gave her a neutral smile that did not get anywhere near his eyes. 'Go on. We'll talk later.'

Shaken, Annis went.

The meeting was an unmitigated disaster. Their key client, the company on whose business their whole year's strategy depended, had been notified over the weekend that they were the subject of a hostile takeover bid.

'I'm sorry,' said the CEO, made brusque by pressure. 'You've got to understand. For now we've got to throw all our energies into fighting off Galloways. If we get away with our tail-feathers, we'll come back to you.'

Even though he had been half expecting it, Roy was stunned into silence. Maybe because she had already endured all the emotional jolts she could sustain that morning, Annis recovered faster.

'Of course,' she said smoothly. 'We quite see that. Don't we, Roy?'

'I suppose so,' he muttered.

'But you may want to look at some strategic analysis to help you fight off Galloways,' she remarked. 'Nothing detailed. Quick and dirty. Comparative advantages and potential, that sort of thing. To persuade shareholders to stay on board.'

The CEO looked at his watch. 'I'll bear that in mind,' he said, clearly preparing to banish them from his thoughts.

Annis stood up and held out her hand.

'Good luck.'

For a moment the man's weary eyes lightened. 'Thanks, Annis.'

Roy opened his mouth.

'We'll be seeing you,' said Annis swiftly. 'Come on, Roy. The man has corporate raiders to repel.'

They left.

On the way down to the ground floor, Roy said in an injured voice, 'I was going to suggest that we completed the first part of our brief.'

'I know you were.'

'So why did you hustle me out?'

Annis stopped dead and looked at him. 'Because he's not going to think about anything like that until after his board meeting,' she said shrewdly. 'I've planted the seed. It will grow or it won't, depending on what his board say. But going at him like a bull in a china shop would just make him so annoyed he'd write us off forever.'

They went out into the grey street. Behind the tower of the Stock Exchange the sky was blue but, down below, the autumn sun did not reach the pavements. Annis shivered.

Then she took a hold of herself. Everyone had reverses. The secret was to deal with them without giving in to despair.

'Come on,' she said with a reasonable assumption of cheerfulness. 'I'll buy you a coffee and we'll think about keeping this ship afloat.'

They found a small coffee shop. City workers were picking up their first coffee of the day, some of them still on their way to work. Annis and Roy retreated to a table in a panelled corner and opened Roy's Filofax on the marble-topped table. They pored over the forward planner.

'I could call S.A.B.,' Roy said at last. 'See if we can pull that forward. And Dene's haven't got back to us. I could chase. What about that architect's practice? Any more work to do there?'

Annis felt heat under her skin. She shook her head. 'I delivered the report this morning.'

'Follow-up?'

She shuddered. 'Most unlikely,' she said firmly.

'Really? But I thought you said it was a mess.'

'It is. I e-mailed you the report yesterday.'

Roy nodded. 'I printed it off but to be honest I haven't had time to look at it properly. I saw you'd offered him plenty of options, though. Are you sure there's no follow up for us?'

Annis buried her nose in her cappuccino. 'I hope not.'

Roy blinked. 'What?'

Annis pulled herself together and said in her most professional tone. 'I very much doubt it. Konstantin Vitale treats his business like his personal fiefdom. If he likes something, it gets done. If he doesn't, nobody even thinks about it again. He isn't going to change.'

And I'm not going to have to face him over a desk remembering what it was like to be in his arms.

Roy was disappointed but philosophical 'Oh, well, if he changes his mind, we've got plenty of spare capacity.'

'He won't,' said Annis. She crossed her fingers under the table.

But she was out of luck.

Konstantin summoned her back the next day. She put on her smartest suit and gold Arabic earrings her father had brought her from the Gulf once. Earrings always made her feel as if she was on stage. It was a boost her confidence needed, face to face with a cool and impeccably turned out Konstantin.

This time, thought Annis distracted, she believed his head office was in Italy. When he did understated elegance he did it a hundred and fifty per cent.

His cordiality was intimidating. He ushered her into his office as if she were a visiting princess and summoned up coffee.

'Hold all calls,' he told Tracy. 'Ms Carew and I have a lot to discuss.'

Annis cleared her throat. 'I really think it would be helpful for your colleagues to sit in.'

Konstantin waved the suggestion away. 'Later.'

He was beautifully shaved and combed this morning. So why did Annis keep thinking of his chin dark with a day's growth of beard and his hair all over the place? She wrenched her wayward thoughts back into line.

Tracy left, closing the door behind her. Konstantin looked at Annis broodingly.

'This,' he said, indicating her bound report, 'is not what I was expecting.'

Annis almost collapsed with relief.

Relief? Ridiculous!

But she was not ready to talk about what had happened between them and she was deeply suspicious that Konstantin Vitale would see nothing wrong with mixing business and a dissection of personal awareness of chemistry,

'No?' she said at last.

He got up. Annis tensed. But he was only moving restlessly round the room.

'I thought you'd tell me to change the colour scheme and put a potted palm in the ladies' loo. Not sack half the staff.'

'And that,' she said calmly, 'is exactly what I expected.'

Kosta looked at her. She looked back.

It was extraordinary how she changed, he thought. If he touched her—if he so much as teased her gently—she got flustered and started knocking things over. But challenge her on her work and she did not bat an eyelid. She had come in here taut as a spring, though. Was that because she thought he would touch her, then?

The idea intrigued him.

'Overreaction,' said Annis. 'I did not tell you to sack anyone.' Annis leaned forward and picked up her report. She waved it at him. 'If you had read this properly, instead of skimming through it in the back of your limo this morning, you would see exactly what I say.'

I could touch her right now. Ms Carew you're lovely when you're angry. Kosta tried to smile at the thought. It still brought him out in a cold sweat.

Annis did not notice. 'Vitale and Partners is the classic organic company. Works fine while it's small—everyone chats, knows what's going on, and comes back to the hive at the end of a task. But—are you listening to me?—but you are not small any more. You don't chat with everyone. It's physically impossible.'

She looked wonderful on her crusade, he thought. Full of fire and determination. Now all he had to do was get her to switch her focus to Vitale the man and the world would shift off its axis with the force of it.

He struggled to concentrate on the business in hand.

'E-mail…' She stood up. 'How many e-mails do you get in a day? Or the design team? Or Tracy for that matter?'

Annis felt wonderful. She knew her subject and she was in control of her material. She soared.

'So, as I see it, you've got two choices,' she said, as if he had never kissed her senseless or made her walk her flat at four in the morning. 'You can downsize. Or you can get bigger—in which case you need a bit of structure, some clear responsibilities and a lot of delegation.'

'I delegate.'

'No, you don't,' she contradicted calmly. 'They don't even call in someone to patch the roof until you get back to the office.'

He was looking at her strangely. She did not care.

'It's all there. Read it. Not just the appendix.'

She closed the report with a bang and slapped it back on his desk. She was breathing hard. She was also, she found, shaking with rage. At least she hoped it was rage.

For a moment he said nothing. Then, slowly, 'Wow.'

'You,' said Annis, winding down, 'asked me.'

She ignored the coffee and picked up some mineral water, swigging it straight from the bottle.

'Yes, I did, didn't I?' Konstantin considered her thoughtfully for a moment. 'You really tell it like it is, don't you?'

'That's what you pay me for.'

He digested that in silence for a moment. 'And you always tell the truth? No fudging to keep important clients sweet?'

Annis gave a wry smile. 'That hasn't been a problem so far.'

'Hmm. So I've got exactly the same treatment as everyone else.'

She worked hard not to remember that kiss in the limousine. Or yesterday morning when there had been no kiss but the very air between them had been as thick and dangerous as a magic forest.

'Of course.'

He sent her a shrewd look. Annis was aware of him all through her body. She avoided meeting his eyes. Now that she wasn't taking his company to pieces she felt all that stored electricity sizzling in the air between them again.

If he mentions the word chemistry, I'll probably go up in a puff of smoke, she thought with painful self-mockery.

But he didn't. Instead he smiled.

She went hot.

His smile widened.

'I didn't skip straight to the appendix. I read all the stuff that said the partnership was overstretched and non-selective.'

'Oh.'

'And I agree.'

Annis blinked.

'Only I have to keep on working to bring in the paying customers. I haven't got time for all that.' He nodded at the report.

Annis smiled tolerantly. 'So you're not going to do a thing about it,' she said, unsurprised.

He gave a soft laugh. 'So you'd better come in and do it for me.'

'*What?*'

'And the sooner the better.'

Annis felt as if the bottom had fallen out of the world and she was in free fall. She stared at him in undisguised horror.

He raised his eyebrows. From the gleam that came into his eyes, Annis thought he was beginning to enjoy himself.

'Can't leave a job half done,' he said virtuously.

Annis regarded him with the deepest suspicion. 'Are you playing some game?'

Konstantin looked hurt. 'Would I?'

'Yes, if it got you what you wanted,' Annis whipped back sharply. She heard what she had said and blushed. 'I didn't mean that you wanted me. I mean, I did, but not like that. I mean...' She floundered into silence and her colour deepened.

Konstantin watched her with deep enjoyment. 'Want to rewind that one?'

I'd like to rewind this whole conversation.

Annis took another gulp from the bottle of mineral water while her mind took rapid stock. She recalled what she had said to Roy. Nothing would change in Vitale and Partners unless Konstantin changed it personally. She straightened her shoulders.

'This company is your baby. You make every decision. No one else can do anything unless you tell them to. If you want to change—and frankly I'm unconvinced—you change it.'

There was a pause.

'Turning me down, Annis?' he said softly.

She did not meet that one head-on. Instead she met his eyes indignantly.

'Do you want to change?'

He hesitated. 'Maybe I'm already changing.'

Another pause, longer and more complicated. This time Annis found her unease was more than embarrassment. Was he—could he be—serious? And, if so, was he talking about work alone? Or...?

I can't handle this. I don't know where I am with this man. I've got to get out of here.

Annis picked up her briefcase. 'Read the report,' she advised. 'Properly, this time. If you're serious, we can talk about implementation once you've decided which of my strategic solutions you want to go for. Until then—' she drew a shaky breath '—just keep out my hair, OK?' Her voice very nearly broke.

'Annis—'

But she shook her head and pushed past him before he could detect her confusion. Or the naked hunger.

CHAPTER SIX

'WE'RE saved! Vitale wants us to do a follow up implementation scheme.' Roy was beaming. Annis felt her heart rock like a moored boat at the first sign of a tidal wave.

'You mean, Vitale wants me to do a follow-up,' she corrected in a hollow voice.

'Same difference. I can keep after the other clients. You make sure the short term cash flow keeps up. Have you billed him for the first report yet, by the way?'

'No.' She hesitated, then said in a rush, 'Look, Roy, I'm really not sure about this one.'

They were sitting in Roy's untidy office above the garage, converted from a guest bedroom when he'd started the partnership with Annis. In the distance his wife called out to one of the children to put their outdoor shoes on. It was a reminder Annis did not need that Roy had a wife and children to support.

'You can handle it,' he said, now bracingly.

Annis was dry. 'Can I?'

'Never met a client yet you couldn't talk round. *And* he's asked for you.'

'Quite,' muttered Annis.

But Roy, scrolling through the client entries on his screen, did not notice.

'If you've done your billed timesheets, I'll put the account in for you, if you like,' he offered.

Annis sighed. He swung round, suddenly paying attention.

'Look, I know you don't like the guy but this is work, love. We can't afford to turn it down.'

She bit her lip, looking away.

'Do you know how many partnerships collapse in the first

105

eighteen months because they get the cash flow wrong? This is a gift.'

The partnership had been Roy's idea in the first place. He had shown a lot of confidence in Annis by asking her to join him and she owed him for that. Besides, he had more to lose than she had and they both knew it. Annis gave a long sigh.

'I know. All right, I'll do it.'

Roy's conscience stirred. 'He's worked for your dad, hasn't he? If you're not happy, why don't you ask him how to handle Vitale?'

Annis nodded slowly. 'That's a good idea. I might just do that.'

Her father was surprised and rather touchingly flattered to be asked for advice. But his diary was clearly full to bursting.

'Never mind. I'll get through somehow. I usually do,' said Annis, trying to be cheerful.

Something in her voice must have struck a chord in Tony.

'Breakfast,' he said. 'Savoy. Seven tomorrow.'

Annis was prompt but Tony was already there at a table in the window. He stood up when he saw her threading her way through the tables.

'I've ordered you porridge and eggs Benedict,' he said, kissing her briskly. 'Your stepmother said you were looking peaky and I ought to feed you well. She sends her love by the way. Told me to ask about some boyfriend but I've forgotten his name.'

'Good thinking, Dad.' Annis was dry. 'Carry on forgetting.'

He looked at her hard. 'You know your own business best. Now, tell me what you're doing for Kosta Vitale.'

She did, succinctly.

'Mmm.' He poured himself more coffee and swirled sugar round in it. 'You think he's going to give you the run-around.' He looked up, sharp as an arrow. 'Professionally or personally?'

Annis caught her breath. Of course, that was why her father was a self-made millionaire. That knife-like cutting through the undergrowth to the root of a problem was his greatest strength.

She answered carefully. 'I'm afraid the two are intertwined.'

He pulled a face. 'Well, I can't advise you on that,' he said ironically.

'But how did you get on with him? I had the impression at dinner that it was not entirely—er—harmonious.'

Her father gave a crack of laughter.

'Well, he's an awkward cuss and stubborn as hell. He likes to win. Kept telling me he had to consider the people who had to look at my building as well as everyone who used it. The guy who was paying seemed to come at the bottom of the list. So we had a bout or two.'

'Who won?'

He stirred his coffee vigorously. 'About fifty-fifty.'

Annis knew her father. That meant that Vitale must have won more often. So even Tony Carew, captain of industry, couldn't get the better of him. Her heart sank. How was she supposed to keep control of the situation with Konstantin if even her father could not?

'Look,' he said abruptly, 'I'm not a woman and I don't know a damned thing about the man's private life. But I know you. You'll be all right as long as keep your head down and do your job.'

Annis was unconvinced and it showed.

Tony put his knife and fork down and took her hand in uncharacteristic encouragement.

'You're an expert. He respects expertise. Trust in that and don't get tangled up in personalities.'

'Easier said than done.'

He squeezed her fingers bracingly. 'You've been doing it for years. Every cocktail party your stepmother gave. You can do it. Melt into the background. Wear camouflage gear.'

Annis laughed. 'Yes, I can do that.'

'Just don't ever take him on head to head.'

But could she do that? Would Konstantin Vitale let her?

She did not voice her doubts to her father, though. He would not know what she was talking about.

'Thanks, Dad. You've been brilliant.'

He scanned her face. 'I'm proud of my clever daughter,' he said gruffly. 'Don't let the bastard wind you up. You can handle him.'

Thus encouraged, Annis marched into Vitale and Partners next morning wearing the best camouflage she could manage, her drabbest suit and most severe hairstyle. And repeating a silent mantra, *Don't take him on head to head. Don't take him on head to head.*

Konstantin Vitale met her in the reception area. If Annis had been of a suspicious turn of mind, she would have said he was lying in wait for her. He took in her appearance in one comprehensive blink. His mouth quirked wickedly.

'Hi, gorgeous.'

Don't take him on head to head.

Annis breathed hard. 'May I have a word in private, Mr Vitale?'

'Just what I was thinking myself.'

And he flung the door to his office open with great ceremony.

Annis was almost certain that she heard Tracy at the reception desk giggle. It did not improve her mood. Almost before the door was closed she swung round on him.

Don't take him on... It was no good. If she let him get away with this sort of blatant teasing at the very start of the assignment, how far would he go by the end? Identify problems early and deal with them at once. That was the management consultant's creed.

So, dealing with the problem, or so she told herself, Annis banged a hand down on his desk. 'You can just cut that out.'

'Excuse me?'

'I won't have you "Hi, gorgeousing" me,' said Annis furiously. 'It's not respectful. And it gives the staff the wrong idea.'

'But what sort of idea does it give you?' asked Konstantin, interested.

Annis eyed him broodingly. And told him the truth.

'It fills me with an almost irresistible urge to poke you in the eye.'

'Excellent.'

'No, it's not excellent. It's violent and childish and I very much resent it.'

He grinned.

'Which is why,' said Annis very, very calmly, 'you and I have got to come to an agreement on this.'

'Are you proposing to me?'

Her calm rocked dangerously. 'In your dreams,' Annis retorted before she could stop herself. She took several calming breaths. 'Look, I will come and work for you. I will work through the possible strategies with you. I will put this place on a viable footing. But I will *not*—not under any circumstances—take any more of your nonsense.'

Konstantin looked delighted. 'My nonsense,' he echoed, rolling it round his tongue like a fine wine. 'Do you have great-aunts, by any chance?'

Annis had realised the moment she had said it that it sounded unbearably pompous. Why did he always manage to wrong foot her? Why could she never learn to deal with his teasing without losing her rag? She dealt with other people well enough.

'You know what I'm talking about,' she said, despairing.

He gave her a beautiful smile. 'You want me to keep my hands off you,' he interpreted.

To her fury Annis flushed to her eyebrows. *'No—'*

'No?'

'Well, yes, of course,' she corrected, blushing harder. 'That goes without saying. I'm trying to be professional.' Appalled, she heard her own voice: it was close to breaking. She gritted her teeth. 'Can't you do the same?'

There was an odd silence while he watched her from narrowed eyes. Then, unexpectedly, he gave a quick, very foreign shrug. It was as if the game had suddenly lost its entertainment value.

'OK. Professional as you like.' He paused. 'At work.'

'What?'

'It's all here,' he said, flourishing her own report at her. It was, Annis saw, well-thumbed. 'Work time. Non-work time. Presumably even you aren't going to tell me what to do in my non-work time?'

'No, but—'

'Fine,' he said briskly. 'Professional in the office. Outside it, you take your chances.'

It was the start of one of the most stressful few days in Annis's life. In the office Konstantin Vitale was as good as his word. Well, almost. If he prowled round her like a tiger circling its prey, if his eyes were full of secret laughter every time he looked at her, if his every courteous gesture was thinly disguised mockery—well, nobody else in the partnership seemed to see it.

But on one thing he was adamant.

'No more, Mr Vitale,' he said firmly. 'Kosta.'

'Professional?' Annis said wearily.

'Sure. Everyone calls me Kosta. Here in London, in Milan, in New York. Even my lawyer calls me Kosta and no one treats me more professionally than he does. You should see the bills.'

Annis gave up. 'OK. Kosta it is.'

She thought he would revel in his triumph but he did not. Instead he said quietly, 'Didn't hurt, did it?'

And when she looked at him she found his eyes were oddly bleak.

By Friday night, Annis was exhausted. Kosta came in from a site meeting to find her drooping at his desk and took decisive action.

'Get your coat. I'm driving you home.'

'No,' said Annis, shooting upright.

'Don't be a fool. You're bushed.'

'I can carry on for a couple of hours.' Annis struggled to focus on the files open on the desk.

'Not in time I'm paying for, you can't,' he said grimly. 'What sort of quality control do you management consultants use, for God's sake?'

Annis had to admit he had a point. She brushed a weary hand through her loosened hair. For once she forgot to cover the scar that ran from brow to hairline. Forgot, at least, until she saw the sudden intent look on Kosta's face.

'What's that?'

Her fingers flew to the ugly mark. Too late. She turned away, shaking her hair forward.

'I'll just pack up and—'

He crossed the room in two swift strides.

'You've hurt yourself. Let me see.'

He took hold of her and turned her to face him. Annis strained away but he would not be gainsaid. His fingers brushed away the soft hair, found the puckered skin, traced it gently, paused...

'How did this happen?'

Annis twitched her head out of his hold and stepped away. 'A long time ago.'

He did not try and bring her back but he watched her narrowly. 'I can see that. How?'

Don't think about the scar. Don't think about anything but work. Do what you have to do and then go on to the next thing. Just don't stop. Don't remember. Don't think.

Annis did not look at him. She put her notes to one side and closed files neatly. In a couple of the older ones, she carefully marked her place with small Post-its that obtruded like dividers to show her where to start tomorrow. She knew her way round the newer files too well to have to bother with marking anything, she thought.

He stopped her by putting a hand over both hers and holding them still on top of the files.

'How? Did someone hurt you?'

Annis swallowed. 'I fell off my horse into a motorbike,' she muttered.

He took her by the chin and turned her face up to him. He trailed a gossamer stroke along the ugly scar, his eyes intent.

'Must have hurt.'

Annis was surprised. It was a long time since she had thought about the pain of the accident. If she had ever thought about it.

'Not so much,' she said more easily. 'At first I was too shocked and then they pumped a load of anaesthetic into me.'

And while I was high as a kite on painkillers I heard my mother saying, 'Her face is ruined. I can't bear to look at it.' And after that she left us.

'How old were you?' he said, still gentle, and so quiet she could hardly hear him.

She had not thought about that for a long time either. She shrugged. 'Nine. Maybe ten.'

He was incredulous. 'And you've still got a hang-up about a tiny scar all these years later?'

'Her face is ruined. I can't bear to look at it.'

'Not so tiny,' said Annis with suppressed rage. 'It made—' She stopped dead.

'It made—?'

'Nothing.'

'Don't do that,' he said sharply.

Annis jumped. 'Do what?'

'The sponge act.'

She did not understand him. 'Sponge?'

'You mop up everything that anyone says and you just *absorb* it. You did it at your parents' house. I watched.'

His quietness, she now realised, masked a rampaging fury. Bewildered, she watched as he banged his fist down on the desk.

'You don't show anything. You just hold it all inside.'

Annis froze. How closely had he watched her? She felt her heart twist in her breast. But her face, as she had trained it to, stayed impassive.

He did not even try to hide his mounting frustration. 'It's crazy. You know it. I know it.'

Annis caught her breath.

Even so small a sign of reaction seemed to mollify Kosta. He said more calmly, 'All this suppression is unhealthy. And,' he added with another little eddy of exasperation, 'it makes it bloody impossible for anyone to get near you.'

Annis was silenced.

'So, let's run this one again shall we? When did you get that scar? And what happened to give you this hang-up?'

But Annis had had enough. 'I'll get my coat.'

She did, giving him a wide berth as she opened the cupboard door. Slightly to her surprise, Kosta neither exploded with temper nor tried to take hold of her again. But his expression did not restore her peace of mind.

'One day,' he said softly, 'you will tell me.'

It sounded like a private promise to himself, one he was determined to keep.

In spite of her warm winter coat, Annis shivered.

She tried to insist on taking a taxi but it was hopeless. For one thing he did not listen. For another, on a cold, wet, autumn evening with the theatres about to start all round the West End, every taxi she saw was occupied. She gave up and went with him to his car.

'What happened to the chauffeur-driven?'

He looked surprised. 'It's rented. I only use it from time to time.'

He held the door open for her. Annis slipped inside and was instantly assailed by the smell of leather and something sharp and piny like a Scottish woodland. It was strangely familiar.

Unsettled, she said more sharply than she intended, 'You mean you use it when you're out to dazzle the impressionable.'

He got in and started the engine. 'I mainly use it to pick me up from the airport,' he said equably. He pulled out of the dark mews into the main thoroughfare. 'Or sometimes if I'm going from meeting to meeting in central London. It beats the endless search for a parking place.'

Annis was slightly ashamed of herself. 'I can see that,' she admitted. 'I decided not to replace my car for that very reason.'

He glanced at her sideways. 'But it's always easier to think the worst of me, hmm?'

Annis did not answer that. Instead she said, 'Do you keep a car in every port?'

'No. Nor a girl, either, if that's what you were going to ask next.'

'I wasn't,' Annis assured him sweetly, though of course she had been. 'I was going to ask if you found it difficult switching about between left- and right-hand drive.'

'No,' he said. 'Not as long as there's plenty of traffic.'

'Doesn't that make it worse?'

'No. When the traffic is nose to tail you don't try and drive on the wrong side of the road.'

Annis gave a choke of laughter. 'That hadn't occurred to me,' she admitted.

He smiled but didn't answer. He was concentrating on easing the car through a maze of single direction lanes. In the rush-hour traffic he was driving with precision and a cool lack of impatience that Annis would not have expected.

'Do you like driving?' she asked eventually, as they left the congestion of Hyde Park Corner behind.

'I suppose. I like to keep my options open. You can't do that without wheels.'

That was much more what she'd expected. Annis relaxed. She did not like the way Kosta kept disconcerting her. It was good to know that she had got him right in that, at least.

'So what do you do when you are in your other homes?'

'Rent in New York. Share in Sydney. Use the office runabout in Milan.'

Share? Annis opened her mouth to ask him who he shared with and closed it almost as once. None of my business, she told herself firmly.

Only—what sort of relationship would you have to have with someone to share a car with them? Close, she thought.

Really close. Like, you would have to be certain that you wouldn't want to use the car at the same time. Or that you were always going to go to the same places. Like lovers would.

She pulled her collar up round her ears, suddenly chilled.

I know nothing about him. Tracy says he has a different girlfriend every month. But what if he has one special girl in Sydney? Tracy would not necessarily know.

And then another thought struck her. *What does it matter to me if he has?*

She pulled her coat close at the throat and held it.

'Cold? I'll turn the heating up.'

He flicked the glimmering control panel and a swathe of warm air curled seductively round her ankles. In spite of herself, Annis released her death grip on her coat collar.

'I guess I'm just tired.'

'I'm not surprised. You really don't seem to have any switch-off mechanism at all. Don't you ever blow up?' He sounded irritated.

Annis relaxed further. She was more comfortable with Kosta irritated than Kosta all warm and concerned.

'I'm a work horse,' she said with a touch of smugness. 'Just keep on plodding on.'

That did nothing to abate his irritation. 'You need a good shaking up.'

'No, I don't.'

'For your own good,' he said warming to his theme. 'No one should be an automaton at twenty-nine.'

'I'm not an automaton,' protested Annis. She was slightly shaken to discover that he remembered her age so precisely. Of course it was the very first thing she had told him. But he shouldn't have bothered committing it to that phenomenal memory. Why had he?

His next remark told her. 'Your parents think so too.'

She stiffened. She knew that Vitale's biggest project was Carew's new head office on the river bank. Kosta had visited the site only that morning. But he had never mentioned that he had bumped into her father at any of the planning meetings. And there was no reason at all why he should meet Lynda.

'My parents?' she echoed, several degrees of frost in her voice.

'All work and no play. That's what Lynda said. She wasn't even sure that you were coming to this fling of hers tomorrow night.'

Annis felt her spine lengthen and mutate into pure steel.

'You're going?' The frost had just turned polar.

He did not look at her. 'I've been on the guest list longer than you. Lynda bounced me into buying a ticket weeks ago. In fact—' He stopped.

Annis was so angry with herself that she did not notice. Why on earth had she not asked Lynda who else was going in the Carews' party? She was so *stupid*.

She came back to the present with a jerk. He was musing aloud.

'You know, before I met you I thought you were one of those luxury ladies who try on careers for size. Rich chick messes up; Daddy buys off everyone who got hurt, and on they go, leaving the injured to lick their wounds.'

His voice was rueful but Annis thought she detected a hint of bitterness. She would put money on there being a rich chick who'd left him somewhere in his past. Against her will, she felt a surge of something like sympathy.

He was not aware of it, pursuing his own thoughts. 'Only, you don't pretend, do you? You're the real thing. Management consultant to your unpainted fingertips.'

Annis stuffed her hands in her pockets.

'Oh, yes, you're professional. In spades. Trouble is, you're nothing else.' No doubt at all now. The bitterness was steaming off him like the sybaritic in-car heating.

'Thank you for the character analysis,' said Annis with awful politeness.

They were at the entry to the private road that led to her block. He turned the car and coasted to the barrier, winding down the window to reply to the duty porter's disembodied query.

'Vitale bringing home Miss Carew.'

The barrier rose at once.

'It only takes one visit for the porters to recognise you,' said Annis, not best pleased.

'Charm,' said Kosta lightly.

She snorted. The car swished through the barrier, almost silent except for the tyres on the wet tarmac.

He smiled faintly. 'The charm of a good story backed by hard cash. It was not easy to persuade them to mop up that flower arrangement.'

'What did you tell them?' demanded Annis, suddenly suspicious.

'You wouldn't want to know.'

'But—'

He flicked a glance sideways at her.

'Be honest. You don't really want to know about anything that's out of your control, do you?'

The car slid silently up to the brightly lit entrance and stopped. Annis swung round in her seat. In spite of the faint smile, his eyes were not amused.

He forestalled her before she could speak. 'You're not going to ask me in. I know.'

For a moment Annis was almost sufficiently annoyed to invite him. For a moment. Almost. Only then she saw the calculated strategy behind it.

'You think you know me so well,' she flared.

If he was disappointed at the failure of a stratagem, he did not show it. He shrugged.

'Doesn't take much. For instance, I'd put money on you already working on your excuse for tomorrow evening.'

Annis flung her door open. 'Then you don't know me as well as you think,' she flung at him. 'I keep *my* promises.'

The contrived smile died. 'And what does that mean?'

'Some people don't.'

'You mean me,' he interpreted. 'When did I ever break a promise?'

Annis thought of all the messages she had seen on his e-mail files. Woman after woman wondering why he wasn't calling, where he was, what she had done... Her anger was like a fizzing firework in the civilised confines of the luxury car.

'*Some* people,' she said savagely, 'take good care not to make promises in the first place.'

She banged her way out of the car without looking back.

All very satisfying at the time, but it left Annis with a problem. She could not, now, get out of going to the ball without climbing down in the face of Kosta's blatant challenge. Which, of course, was out of the question.

So what she had to do was knock his eyes out! She promised it to herself ferociously. A professional and nothing else, indeed! She would *make* him see exactly what else she was. She would make Konstantin Vitale grovel if she never did anything else. It would be a blow for all those women in his obsolete files.

It was only when she simmered down that she realised the practical difficulties of turning herself into an instant knockout. She spent a strenuous morning cruising the smarter shops. Nothing worked. Her panic-level rose. Despairing, she returned home and was reluctantly contemplating a range of feeble excuses after all when Gillie Larsen rang.

'What's wrong?' said her friend at once.

'A small case of despair,' said Annis ruefully. 'I've bitten off more than I can chew.'

'About time,' said Gillie obscurely.

'What?'

'Never mind. Explain.'

Annis did.

Gillie was, as always, immensely practical. 'Sounds like a job for style counsellor Larsen. Get yourself down here and we'll have a head-banging session.'

She went. Gillie, devastating in leather trousers and a figure-hugging short-sleeved top, stepped through a floor of toys and marched her straight to the spare room.

'Who? What? Where?' she said briskly. 'And why is he worth all this bother?'

'He isn't,' said Annis, weaving her way less daintily. A plastic fire engine crunched under her foot. 'Oh, sorry.'

'All flesh is grass,' said Gillie, unmoved. 'Likewise plastic vehicles. Even rich kids have to learn that.' She waved Annis to an elaborately flounced dressing stool. 'Sit.' She narrowed her eyes measuringly and turned to a stuffed cupboard. 'Why the effort if he isn't worth the bother?'

'I work for him.'

'You work for lots of people.'

Annis gave a reluctant laugh. She was remembering a little too clearly. 'He said I was a management consultant to my unpainted fingertips,' she said in a rush.

Gillie blinked. 'You're joking, right?'

'No.'

'And you *minded*?'

'Yes, I—' Annis caught up with the implications of Gillie's tone. 'Of course I minded,' she said heatedly. 'Wouldn't you?'

'Oh, I would,' agreed Gillie.

'Well, then—'

There was a brief pause. Then Gillie seemed to pull herself together.

'Right. One management consultant, fully transformed. We can do that.'

Gillie ran her finger along the rail. 'If you're ending the evening together you'll want something he can slip you out of without a degree in advanced engineering.'

Annis swallowed. By a supreme effort of will she neither blushed nor allowed her mind to dwell on the too easily conjured up picture of Kosta slipping her out of anything. Nevertheless she was aware of a faint uneasiness at what she had unleashed.

'Don't get carried away.'

'I won't. You, on the other hand, might,' Gillie said. She sounded pleased.

Selecting a couple of hangers, she threw their contents carelessly onto the bed behind her. 'A woman has to be prepared for every eventuality.'

'Not that one,' said Annis firmly.

Gillie turned bright eyes on her. 'Why not?'

'Well—er—'

'You want to knock his eyes out? You gotta take the consequences.'

'Maybe this was a bad idea,' said Annis, getting up.

Gillie pursed her lips, considering something in fuchsia. 'Why?'

'These—' Annis gestured at the fabulous pile of silks and velvets '—are much too glamorous for me. I couldn't keep up.'

'So why all this concern about what you wear in the first place?' demanded Gillie shrewdly.

Annis gave a gusty sigh and said simply, 'I got mad.'

'Fine. Stay mad,' Gillie advised. 'I've been wanting to do this for *years*. You have a figure to die for. It's criminal the way you waste it.'

'Th-thank you,' said Annis, startled.

'That was not a compliment.' She turned back to her wardrobe, tapping her teeth. 'Now, what about chestnut satin?'

In spite of herself Annis looked and squawked in alarm. 'I can't wear that. It hasn't got any front.'

'That's the point. You provide the front.' Gillie turned the hanger round with a flourish.

Annis made a discovery. 'And less back. I couldn't wear that. I'd be terrified.'

Gillie raised her eyebrows. 'That'll be a culture shock. You'll get used to it.'

Annis shook her head. 'No way. That's the sort of thing Bella wears, not me.'

'It would knock his eyes out, though,' said Gillie, wheedling.

'And give me a nervous breakdown.' Annis put the bronze dress down with determination. 'Do you think there's anything in there that will do?'

Gillie grinned. 'Is the world round? Brace yourself. I am going to make you *irresistible*.'

She did not quite do that. But after a kaleidoscope half-hour of lime-greens and petrol-blues, leather and velvet, silk and fur, Annis was at last stunned into accepting an outfit that, Gillie assured her, would drive any man wild with desire.

'You mean it doesn't look as if it was designed for the management consultants' annual bun-fight?' said Annis, concentrating on essentials.

'Absolutely not. All I have to do is take the hem up a bit.'

'Why? It looks fine.'

Gillie smiled pityingly. 'It will spoil the transformation scene if you go up the grand staircase and fall flat on your face because you catch your toe in your skirt. Leave it to me.' She pushed her towards the door of the apartment. 'I'll bring it up. Go and do what normal women do when they're going on a hot date.'

'It's not a date...'

'Sure. And you're not going with the laser-tongued sex god, either,' said Gillie tolerantly. She thrust Annis out of the door. 'Go and have a scented bath and paint your nails. You know you want to. That'll really show him.'

Annis did.

As it turned out, that was unwise.

Gillie did not deliver the dress herself. Instead she entrusted a large shiny purple carrier bag to the porters to deliver. A short note was attached.

We've taken the kids out for pizza, so we'll be out when you leave for your party. Herewith the dress and my gold

choker in case you haven't got anything that will do. I
guarantee irresistible. Enjoy!

Puzzled, Annis pulled aside tissue paper. She had half expected Gillie to come up and help her dress and was a little hurt that her friend had not thought of it.

But as soon as she drew out the dress she knew why Gillie had done a bunk. It was the gleaming chestnut satin. All the soothing effects of a neroli-scented bath exploded as Annis swore and started to rip her way through her own wardrobe, knowing that it was hopeless.

She rang Lynda.

'Don't tell me. You're not coming. Everyone said you wouldn't turn up when it came to it.'

About to say exactly that, Annis paused. *Everyone* had said that? Including Kosta Vitale, no doubt. Well, she was not going to give him the satisfaction of predicting her actions correctly.

'I'll be there,' said Annis between her teeth. 'I may a bit late, though.'

'I'll leave your ticket at the entrance,' promised Lynda.

So rather more than an hour later Annis squared her shoulders and walked into the grand ballroom of the eighteenth-century house that Lynda's committee had hired for their ball. There were great branches of free-standing candelabra in the marble entrance hall and the scent of hot-house lilies everywhere. Intricate eighteenth-century plasterwork had been spectacularly gilded and the pillars seemed to shimmer in the candlelight.

But Annis was beyond noticing her exotic surroundings. She had never felt so self-conscious in her life.

Gillie's dress was cut on the cross. That meant that when Annis walked or danced it would swirl beautifully but when she stood still it clung. How it clung!

Bella was the first to see her. She rushed over.

'Brains, you look *fantastic*.' She sounded stunned. 'I wouldn't have recognised you.'

Annis grimaced. 'That makes two of us.'

Then she took in Bella's own appearance and blinked. Bella was wearing black—high-necked, long-sleeved and a filigree butterfly in her hair.

'Looks as if we've changed style.'

Bella grinned. 'Don't you believe it.'

Annis grimaced. 'I don't feel like myself at all.'

'But it's great. Don't you feel wonderful?'

Annis considered. 'I feel,' she said precisely, 'like a very old wall that has just been spray-painted dayglo orange. You can see every bump and bulge.'

Bella giggled. 'Yup,' she said in congratulatory tones. 'You certainly can.'

A couple that Annis knew from her childhood walked past. Normally they would have stopped and chatted for several minutes. Tonight, though, the woman gave her a wintry smile and speeded up, tightening her grip on her husband's arm. His eyes never rose above Annis's cleavage.

'First blood of the evening,' Bella murmured in her ear.

Annis resisted the temptation to check her swathed apology for sleeves. They were set at an angle and were cleverly designed to look as if they were falling off, presumably to be followed by the whole dress.

'Everyone is staring,' she hissed out of the corner of her mouth.

'That's my girl,' said Bella, pleased.

Annis was wearing her mother's ruby choker. It was old-fashioned but the crimson stones made her skin look impossibly white and soft. Now she fussed with its single blood-red teardrop. It was designed to rest in the hollow of her throat but the beat of her pulse kept jumping it off centre.

'Don't fidget with that.'

'But I—'

'Look spectacular,' said Bella generously. 'Now, forget it and concentrate. Enjoying yourself is a serious business.'

Something in her tone made Annis look at her sharply. 'Something wrong?'

'Wrong? What could be wrong? My brainy sister looks like a million dollars and we have a whole evening of tombola ahead of us. Come on, I know where our table is.'

There was nothing Annis could say. If something was wrong, Bella was not going to pour her heart out at the start of a dance with several hundred people looking on. Annis promised herself that she would call her sister tomorrow. In the meantime there was the evening to get through.

It was an ordeal following Bella through the crowd to their table. Men stared, some discreetly, some with open avidity. Annis felt hot and oddly apologetic. She wanted to turn to them all and say, This is a disguise. I'm really not like this. Don't be fooled.

But then she got to their table and Konstantin Vitale stood up—and she did not feel like apologising any more. He stared at her without speaking. He stood very still, his face nearly expressionless. But Annis knew those clever features by now and she saw what he wanted to hide: shock; anger; unwanted lust.

Suddenly it was all worth it.

'Good evening,' she said demurely.

She gave him the same courteous, neutral smile she gave everyone else and slid into her seat next to a widget designer from Carews.

There was no opportunity to speak to him during dinner. The tall ballroom had an echo like a mountain cave and it was impossible to project a voice across their table of twelve. So Annis talked to her immediate companions and felt Kosta's eyes on her all the time. It was like a caress, that hot, brooding glance. A caress or a threat. Annis did not know which was the more alarming. Or satisfying.

So she lifted her chin and ignored him. She became more animated with every glass, of course, and every half-heard compliment. Life was, briefly, a blast.

By the time the dancing started she was quite convinced she had won their unacknowledged war. She had knocked his eyes out all right. There would be no more cracks about unpainted fingertips, she thought gleefully.

Almost before the final speech ended he was scraping back his little gilt chair and striding purposefully round the table to her.

'Dance with me.' It was only just an invitation.

The man sitting next to Annis was rueful. 'Beaten to the draw. Maybe you'll let me have a dance later?'

'Don't count on it,' said Kosta before she could answer.

He took her hand and half dragged her between the tables, some of which were still being cleared away for the dancing. In front of the tiny area of floor exposed so far, the band was playing something bouncy. Kosta ignored the rhythm and pulled her into his arms. The material of his dinner jacket was rough against her exposed skin.

'Careful,' said Annis, flushed with social success and champagne. 'I bruise easily.'

She thought he was going to burst into flames.

'What the hell are you doing?'

Annis half lowered her eyelids the way she had seen Bella do and moistened her lips. She even managed a provocative pout, or she thought she did.

'Proving a point. Don't you like it?'

He did not look provoked into further excesses of lust. He looked irritated. 'What point?'

'Management consultants are human too.'

He held her away from him. 'What are you talking about?'

'You said I was professional and nothing else.'

He said slowly, 'And this is to prove me wrong?'

Annis tossed her head and the rubies trembled. 'It's to prove everybody wrong.'

'Oh, my God. What have I started?'

'An avalanche, I hope,' she said sunnily.

The music changed and she let herself be danced away by someone she didn't know. It was very gratifying to see that Kosta did not immediately find another partner. Instead he stood watching her, narrow-eyed, while other dancers bumped off him. Then he seemed to realise where he was and strode from the floor with a determined look on his face. Annis gave a sigh of pure satisfaction.

It was short-lived.

'Annie? *Annie?*'

The voice was vaguely familiar. When she turned she knew why.

'Jamie,' she said hollowly.

Suddenly the gilding dimmed, the scent of lilies was sickly and she had an impending headache.

'I didn't know you were coming. Annie, you look great.' Was there pique in the pleasant voice?

Annis thought, He doesn't want me to look great. He walked out on me and he thinks I ought to be in mourning. He was the glamorous one. He doesn't want the tables turned.

She took a glass of champagne from a passing waiter and took a revivifying draught. 'So do you,' she said politely.

'It's been ages.'

'Has it?' She shook her hair back and gave him a brilliant smile. 'I've been so busy, I didn't notice.'

He relaxed a little. 'Oh, yes, we all know busy, busy Annis. Had your nose to the grindstone?'

A slow fury started to build in Annis. How dared he patronise her like that? How dared he? She'd let him into her life and her home, had loved him without reservation. Had he always been sneering at her secretly?

She widened her eyes and gave an amazingly good imitation of Bella's slowest, sexiest smile.

'Not all the time.'

The band was starting again. Dancers jostled them. Jamie looked round.

'Look, let's go and get a breath of air. Catch up a bit.'

'Fine,' said Annis with totally deceptive amiability.

If he thought he could take her onto the terrace and romance her back into her former trusting quiescence, he was very much mistaken. Annis had a point to make. She drained her glass and acquired another one on her way to the long French windows, in his wake.

The autumn garden had been illuminated for the occasion. There were fairy lights in old mulberry trees and little silvery stars twined through the winter jasmine. The stars blinked on and off.

'Naff,' said Annis loudly.

She felt as if she were on a crusade against everything phoney. Including her ex-fiancé.

Jamie looked rather startled. But he had another point to make altogether. He began to stroke her arm.

'Annie, darling. I couldn't believe it when I saw you this evening,' he said huskily.

Annis nodded. 'Lots of people didn't believe it.' She nodded several times more, then found that it made her feel dizzy and stopped.

'I've missed you.'

He walked his fingers up her arm. Once that caress had made her shiver with delight. Now the only thing that was making her shiver was cold. And it *was* cold. She said so.

'Then let me take you home and warm you up,' said Jamie, never one to let an opportunity go to waste.

He slid the disreputable ruched strap down her arm and kissed her bared shoulder. Annis felt his tongue against her chilled skin and thought, *No*.

She pushed him away. Jamie laughed softly. He had always, she remembered suddenly, liked a bit of opposition. He did not seriously believe any woman could not want to make love with him but he enjoyed overcoming pretend resistance. Suddenly Annis thought, *Is he going to realise that this is not pretend?*

She pushed him away again. Jamie drew a little, excited breath and his arms closed round her so tight she could not breathe. She struggled, but her fragile heel caught in a paving slab and snapped. Annis lurched and grabbed at his shoulder to save herself. Jamie took it for surrender.

'Annie—'

'Let me go,' spat Annis furiously.

'You don't mean that. Darling, you and I were—'

'Washed up a long time ago,' Annis said, prodding at his chest without much effect. Probably because she was also hopping on her uneven shoes. 'Let me *go*.'

And then there was help.

'Now,' said Kosta Vitale, chopping Jamie's arm from her around her as if he might break it.

He spun Annis away from him like a man who had broken up a lot of fights in his time. She staggered and sat down rather suddenly on the coping. After one swift glance he ignored her, placing himself between her and Jamie.

'Go in and get a bucket of coffee,' he said mildly enough. But his body said that he was quite prepared for a fight. Jamie blinked.

'What the—? Who gave you the right to interfere?'

'Annis,' said Kosta briefly.

'Annie?' Jamie's laugh was loud. 'Annie doesn't give men rights.'

'Maybe not,' said Kosta levelly. 'But you walked into the middle of a fight between her and me. I'm sorry if the sexy dress gave you the wrong impression. It was aimed at me.'

Annis leaned against one of the supporting pillars.

'That's not true,' she mumbled.

'And,' concluded Kosta in the same invincibly pleasant tone, 'it's up to me to take her home before she falls out of it entirely.'

CHAPTER SEVEN

WITHOUT waiting for her agreement, Kosta put an arm round her waist and hitched her to her feet. Annis let go of her supporting column reluctantly. She was feeling most peculiar. So peculiar in fact that she barely protested against his high-handed treatment as he marched her along the terrace, half carrying her as the effect of the broken heel made itself felt.

He avoided the seething ballroom. 'Ant heap,' he said with distaste, steering her past its windows.

Instead he took her into a small room at the corner of the house. It turned out to be a library. Table lamps and a roaring fire gave it a soft glow. Several couples had retreated here with their coffee, presumably to avoid the noise of the ball-room. They were sitting comfortably in deep sofas and antique chairs, talking or—in one case that gave Annis a sharp stab of envy—just embracing dreamily as they stared into the fire. No one even looked up as Annis and Kosta came in.

'Romantic,' said Annis scornfully, because something in so much easy intimacy hurt her heart.

Kosta glanced down at her, unsmiling. 'What is wrong with romance?'

'It's fiction. Rose petals and hot air.' She waved a contemptuous hand.

'You speak from personal experience?'

Something about tonight was making Annis abandon her careful discretion. 'Oh, I do. I do indeed.'

'You must tell me about that some time,' he said politely, tugging her after him as he weaved his way between furniture and oblivious couples.

'As if you'd care,' muttered Annis. But not loudly enough for him to hear.

In the marble entrance hall he negotiated her onto a Jacobean settle.

'Wait there. I'll get the car.'

At last Annis began to fight back. 'What if I don't want to go?'

He raised his eyebrows. 'You want to dance on one heel?'

'I could take my shoes off.'

For some reason that made his face darken even more.

'You're twenty-nine years old and you live for your work,' he reminded her in a furious undertone. 'You're not a bare-foot party girl.'

'You're so hidebound,' Annis mocked.

'And you're playing with fire,' he said between his teeth. 'Now sit there and don't move.'

'I ought to say goodbye to my parents.'

'I'll let them know I'm taking you home,' he allowed curtly.

Annis glared. 'I'm not six years old, you know.'

'I'd noticed. Just like every other man here tonight.' He was still curt. 'I hope you enjoyed yourself.'

Annis thought, *Nice that he's the one losing his rag for once.*

'Oh, I did,' she assured him.

There was a seething silence. Startled, Annis almost thought that he might strike out. A delicate statue of Hermes, messenger of the gods, was in his line of fire and she held her breath at its imminent danger.

But the moment passed.

'Wait!' he told her, the single explosive word like a gun-shot.

Then he strode out into the darkness.

Annis sank onto the settle and leaned back into its protective wing. She felt as if she was floating. If this was irresponsibility, she loved it! For once she could abandon her ruthless common sense and leave everything to Kosta's superb competence. She smiled to herself, basking.

'There you are,' said Bella.

Annis's eyes flew open. Her sister was standing in front of her, small face pinched with anxiety.

'I saw Jamie. Did he upset you?'

'No,' said Annis. It was the truth which faintly surprised her.

Bella still looked tense.

'Is something wrong?' said Annis, coming down off her lovely cloud.

Bella's jaw clenched. 'Nothing new.'

'What?'

'I changed my image,' she burst out. 'Toned everything down and bored myself rigid behaving well, and all for what? He hasn't even *noticed*!'

Annis remembered Bella's unknown love object.

'He's here?' she said, surprised.

But Bella was too absorbed in her self-recriminations to notice, far less answer.

'I've turned myself inside out for that man. And he doesn't give a tinker's damn. He doesn't care about anybody. I know what they said. But I thought I could handle it, you know? I thought, He'll care about *me*.'

She stopped abruptly and folded her lips together as if she might cry. Shocked, Annis heaved herself upright and pulled Bella down on the settle beside her. She put a protective arm round her sister.

'He will,' she said, stroking the soft blonde hair. 'Give him time.'

'Time only makes him bored,' Bella said desolately. She rested against Annis for a moment. 'I wish I was like you. I feel so *humiliated*.'

'Oh, love,' said Annis. She felt helpless.

Bella scrubbed a hand over her face and sat up. 'No point in making a fuss. I gave it my best shot.' She gave a watery smile. 'And now I've got to get back to the dance floor and prove I don't give a damn either. Maybe that will do the trick.'

She didn't sound hopeful. But she gave Annis a grateful squeeze and went. Annis watched her straighten her shoulders and prance back into the festivities as if she was born to party and didn't have a care in the world. Annis's heart went out to her.

But then Kosta came running back, his jacket turned up against the rain, and she forgot Bella, forgot everything. There must have been sleet in the rain because some of the ice drops spangled his hair like diamonds. The sheer magnetism of the man struck her like a blow. She got up and limped towards him as if a powerful magnet had been trained on her.

Oh, help! thought Annis.

But she still went.

In the car she could not think of anything to say. Kosta was equally silent, his expression grim. He was driving with a sort of angry meticulousness that made her grateful for the lack of conversation. She was fairly sure that any remark would deteriorate rapidly into a full-blown fight.

Partly because she could not face a battle and partly because she was feeling strange again, she did not resist when he announced that he was seeing her to her door. She let him help her across the car park, but as soon as she was inside she slipped out of the uneven shoes and tossed them in the waste-paper basket in the reception area. The porter—it was the frustrated poet again—waved a conspiratorial hand as the lift doors closed on them.

Annis leaned back against the wall and closed her eyes.

'Yes, you really overdid it tonight, didn't you?' Kosta did not sound sympathetic.

Annis opened her eyes and looked at him with dislike.

'Who made you the thought police?'

'Police!' He was outraged.

'Killjoy,' said Annis with relish.

He eyed her unflatteringly. 'What is it with you? You go from business harpy to wild child with no stops in between. Do you know who you are?'

'Girls just want to have fun,' she said airily.

The lift got to her floor. She got out safely enough but her sheer tights skidded on the deep-pile carpet.

'Damn,' said Annis, lurching into a hard body and dropping her keys.

Their eyes met. Annis felt as if she had been plugged into some solar power source. She fizzed with it at the same time as her head reeled.

She had not the slightest idea if he felt the same. But he felt *something*. She could see that all right. It was there in his eyes, just as it had been when he'd first caught sight of her this evening.

I can make him look like that, thought Annis exultant.

Slowly Kosta restored her to her feet and picked up the keys. His eyes did not leave her face. Annis was dizzy with the intensity of it.

'I'm coming in.' His voice was very quiet. It was not a question.

He inserted the key and opened the door as if he had been doing it all his life. As if he had the *right*.

And she let him.

Inside he found the light which turned on the table lamps and looked round the sitting room. His expression was that of an explorer quartering the North Pole.

'So this is your bolt-hole.'

Annis pulled herself together. 'Yes, it is. And I didn't invite you into it.'

'That's just because you were too surprised. You would have got round to it,' he said superbly. 'And, thank you, yes, I would kill for a coffee.'

'No,' said Annis. She was saying no to a lot more than making him a cup of coffee and they both knew it.

Kosta narrowed his eyes. They looked very green in the shadows that filled the room between the little lamps and the concentrated pool of light at her desk.

'Why not?' he said gently.

Because I don't trust you. Because you're out of my league. Because this is going too fast and I don't know what I'm getting in to...

He strolled around the sitting room, picking up books and

her few ornaments and examining them. Annis watched him on tenterhooks. Kosta saw it. He smiled.

'I'll make a bargain with you,' he said. 'You give me a coffee and I won't psychoanalyse your reading matter.'

Annis hesitated. He was holding a well-thumbed copy of *Jane Eyre*.

'Though it's interesting stuff for a lady who despises romance,' he said softly.

Annis gave in.

'One coffee and then you go.'

'Agreed.'

He gave her a bland smile and flung himself back in the old sofa. She had bought it at auction years ago when she was first looking for furniture, any furniture, and these days she flung an ivory-coloured throw over it. That made it blend in with the rest of the room, all cream and beige with touches of toffee colour to pick up the golden gleam of the polished wooden floor.

It was light and airy and very cool. And, apart from the crowded desk, meticulously tidy.

'I don't know why you keep people out of here,' he said when she brought the coffee back to him. 'You don't give much of yourself away.'

Annis thought of her fantasy bedroom and bit back a smile. She had put her whole heart and soul into that room and no one had ever seen it, not even Jamie, whose departure had precipitated her artistic efforts. Kosta Vitale was certainly not going to.

She said in a neutral voice, 'The place suits me.'

He looked at her narrowly. 'You're laughing at me. What have I said?'

She shrugged. 'Nothing. I didn't invite you in to give me a run-down on what is wrong with my decor.'

'You didn't invite me in at all,' he agreed. He leaned back among the pale cushions and surveyed her. 'Why do I make you nervous, Annis?'

She came back, quick as a whip. 'You don't.'

'But I do. Much more nervous than that guy you were fighting off this evening.'

Annis was silent. It was true.

'Who was he?'

'Just a boyfriend.'

His eyes narrowed. 'Ex-boyfriend?'

It felt like a duel. 'Why?'

'Because the first time we met you told me you didn't date.'

'I wish you wouldn't keep harping on that,' said Annis irritably. 'I told you there was a misunderstanding. I'm sorry about it.'

'Yes, I've seen how true it is. You do date.'

She swallowed. 'Well, sometimes...'

'Proves my point, don't you think? I make you defensive and you take refuge in silly exaggerations.'

Annis did not say anything. He stood up.

'Who is he?'

He was very tall. Why did she keep feeling shocked at how tall he was? She did not like tall men. They gave you a crick in your neck. And those were the good ones. The bad ones used their height to intimidate you...

Kosta doesn't intimidate me. He makes me want to—

Annis's thoughts shuddered to a shocked halt as she realised exactly what he made her want to do.

'What?' she said distractedly.

'This man you date sometimes. Or used to date.' Quite suddenly the accent was back. It made him seem very foreign, like someone who didn't know the local rules. Or wasn't going to abide by them even if he knew them. 'Who is he?' he demanded harshly.

Annis folded her lips together. 'Just a guy.'

He gave her a calculating look, then shrugged. 'I suppose his name is unimportant. Is he the reason you don't date any more?'

'No.'

'Sure? You didn't know he was going to be there and dress yourself up like a fairground to get him back?'

'*No!*' said Annis, revolted. 'And I don't look like a fairground. I just fancied a—er—new look.'

'Good.'

He put down his coffee cup untouched and stood up. Strolling over, he took her own cup away from her and, to her astonishment, took her face between powerful hands.

'A new look, hmm? Well, I'll drink to that. But why stop at the clothes? See what this does for you.'

Her head went back. She was right. Tall men put a strain on your neck. At least until they slid their hands round it, supporting it, and slipped long, sensitive fingers into your hair, while their mouth drove you crazy.

Not raising his head, he whispered, 'Admit it. You deliberately set out to get under my skin tonight, didn't you?'

He trailed one finger down the line of sensitivity at the back of her neck. Annis shivered voluptuously.

'Didn't you?'

'Yes.'

His arms went round her, hard.

'Why?' he murmured against her lips.

'I—don't know.' And she didn't.

'Yes, you do.' His hands were moulding her body restlessly. 'Chemistry. You're getting the hang of it at last.'

'No.' She could not think straight. 'No—'

The cloth of Gillie's dress bunched and stretched and glided under his hands as if he wanted to rub it off. But he did not try to remove it. He was just sensitising her every nerve and reflex. Annis felt her body give up its watchful tension.

So this is surrender.

If he felt like a foreigner, so did she. The Annis she knew would never have dreamed of making love to Kosta Vitale. Even now, she was not at all sure that she was whole-heartedly in favour of it.

At least the careful, sensible part of her didn't want to. But the careful, sensible part had got lost somewhere in the sheer enjoyment of her battle with Kosta. The heady sensation of

being able to make him look at her like that had swamped
every bit of judgement she had ever had.

It was much too late now to get it back. Now he was not
just looking. And nor was she.

Every last inhibition had gone. Annis writhed, trying to
wind herself closer and still closer... He bent his head and
buried his mouth in her neck.

Annis gasped and her senses flamed. His open mouth on
the vulnerable skin was new and frighteningly erotic. And he
felt it. Moving against her, he left her in no doubt of his own
desire.

Annis trembled, not with nerves, though heaven knows she
had never felt like this before, but with the sheer electrical
force of their response to each other.

'Take me to bed,' she said, her voice raw.

He did not ask if she was sure. He did not ask anything at
all. Instead he swung her off her feet like a pirate raider.

'Third door,' gasped Annis, nearly incoherent with longing.

When they got there, she reached out across him and turned
on the lights. He almost dropped her in astonishment.

It was the décor: her private project, her secret indulgence,
the heart of the apartment where the real Annis unfolded and
let herself just be. Even Annis, seeing it for the first time
through the eyes of a newcomer, blinked.

Each wall was entirely covered, floor to ceiling, with a
Canaletto street scene. Annis had designed it, then painted it
herself over some long, lonely evenings. The painting was in
Renaissance pastels, picked out with little flashes of jewel colours in a cloak here, a curtain there. The general impression
was that her bed, with its four striped Venetian gondola poles,
one at each corner, had somehow beached in a Palladian
square by the side of a canal. Between the buildings, with their
balconies and candy-twisted columns, dark alleys ran away to
the distant lagoon, shimmering silver at the horizon.

'You don't do things by halves, do you?' said Kosta in a
stunned voice.

The only furniture in the room was the bed and a dark

antique chair under the window. All the cupboards were hidden behind the street scenes, peopled with a bustling crowd of merchants and street entertainers.

'This is—unexpected.'

'I did it all myself,' she said loudly, too loudly in the quiet room. She wished she had the courage to turn on the Pergolesi mandolin concerto that she had been listening to before she went out. But somehow she did not want to share any more with Kosta than was already inevitable.

She slid out of his arms. He let her go without protest and began to wander round the room. He touched a parrot on the shoulder of a merchant coming up the steps from her scarf drawer. Then moved on to run his fingers down the filmy drapery swathed around the bed.

'Why this?'

Annis shrugged, defensive.

'I was thinking of a boat's sails, I suppose.'

He warmed to the fantasy. 'Or a Renaissance beauty hiding herself from the world's eyes.'

She flinched from the word 'beauty'. 'More likely protecting her skin against the sun.'

'There would be plenty of that,' he agreed.

The Mediterranean sun gleamed out of those murals. But just at the moment it was not visible, because Annis had designed the room to reflect the time of day and currently a star filled sky was on duty. Annis was proud of that ceiling—she had painted an authentic array of Mediterranean stars and wired the lights behind them. She would lie on her bed and listen to lutes and almost feel the spice-scented breezes from the lagoon on her skin.

But she had always done it alone. She had never let anyone else look round her fantasy creation before. Yet here was Kosta Vitale, serial womaniser and her employer to boot, drinking it in—and learning far too much about her in the process.

She retreated to the window, edgy and embarrassed.

Kosta did not seem to notice. He shook his head as if he was trying to clear it.

'Amazing.'

'It wasn't meant to be amazing,' Annis said desolately. 'It was meant to be private.'

Kosta did not notice that either. He was still marvelling. He looked up at the starscape and his lips twitched.

'And this is the woman who had the gall to call a few fairy lights naff.'

Annis jumped. That was what she had said to Jamie. Had Kosta been listening? Following her because he could not bear to be bested?

She folded her arms round herself. She was still shaking with little eddies of lust but it was like reaction after shock. It no longer meant anything. She did not want him to touch her any more. She turned away.

'This was a mistake. I'm sorry.'

Kosta noticed at last. He took a step towards her, registered her reaction and stopped.

At last he said carefully, 'What was a mistake?'

Annis made an embarrassed gesture. 'You. Me. You—here. Everything.'

He came over to her but did not touch her.

'Why?'

'We're very different. Too different.'

She thought he would go then. Or try to seduce her. He did neither. Instead, he sat on the edge of the bed and watched her thoughtfully.

'Different?' he mused. 'Well, I've never tried to go bed in the middle of a Venetian market-place. But I'm willing to learn.'

In spite of herself, Annis gave a small laugh. But she said, 'It's more than that.'

He digested it for a moment.

'Are you sure?'

No, thought Annis, shocked. She was not sure at all. That was just the point. At the ball she had been in a daze of vainglorious delight at having rocked him into awareness. For a few hours she had felt beautiful. More than beautiful. She had felt desirable. Kosta had desired her.

But Kosta Vitale never desired a woman for longer than a month. Annis had seen the e-mails to prove it. So now she had to sober up and listen to her wiser self. Her wiser self told her to keep him at arm's length on any excuse she could muster. Any mention of the real reason—his track record, e-mails and all—would somehow betray her.

She said desperately, 'All that jet-setting. You're so much more sophisticated than I am.'

The green eyes were frankly sceptical.

'That's silly,' Kosta said calmly.

'I mean it.'

He did not move, just shook his head a little as if he had detected her lies and deplored them.

'I'd like you to go, please,' said Annis firmly.

'No, I don't think so,' he returned with equal firmness.

Annis couldn't believe it. This was not playing by the rules with a vengeance! 'What?'

Kosta stood up and came to stand in front of her. He did not touch her. But what good was that when her body swayed towards him in pure instinct?

'We've got this far,' he said levelly. 'If we stop now, how long do you think it will take us to get back to this point?'

Annis fought her instincts. 'Never.'

'Oh, it will happen.' His face was harsh suddenly. 'There's no escaping chemistry like this.'

She was silenced. Wasn't her every pore telling her the same thing?

He said, quite kindly, as if he were a tutor persuading her to take an exam, not an urgent lover desperate to have her in his arms, 'I'm not going to let you run away from this, Annis.'

She met his eyes and saw that he meant what he said. She gave a small sob, half of temper, half of sheer panic.

'You can't stop me,' she said, like a child in a tantrum.

He smiled. 'No. You'll do that.'

He touched her cheek fleetingly. Annis clenched every muscle in rejection.

He wants me now. But in another month he'll be in New York, or wherever, and I'll be back painting murals instead of sleeping. He'll break my heart and he won't even notice.

'No,' she said under her breath, appalled.

The green eyes flickered. But Kosta did not retreat.

He wants me now. And I want him. I've never felt like this. If I send him away now will I ever feel like this again? Will I ever know what it is to desire and be desired? Because I don't know yet.

She looked into his eyes and trembled. He was not making any move on her but she recognised the hunger that was almost a pain. Because she shared it.

He wants me now.

She gave a long sigh and swayed. At last he reached out to her, steadying her with hands that tried to be undemanding and were not.

The hell with tomorrow. I don't care.

Annis walked into his arms.

His height, his strength, his sheer *certainty*, overwhelmed her. She twisted and turned around his body, tearing at his clothes and her own. She was desperate not to think, only to feel. And, for all his assurance, Kosta was no less desperate. His breathing was uneven. Once before she had thought that his hands were only just the civilised side of cruel. Now they were like a vice. And shaking.

Annis heard herself crying out with a need that sounded almost like pain. And Kosta responded—with care, with determination and, ultimately, with a total absorption which filled her with awe. She convulsed, throbbing in every pore. She heard him call her name. Gripping him, she was spiralled into the stars...

Later, he slept. Annis lay in his arms. They were both slick with sweat, every muscle relaxed, but she could not sleep. She was filled with a peace too deep for sleep. She had never felt so cared for. More than that: treasured. Or so safe.

She cupped her hands round his jaw. It was already rough with the darkening beard. She savoured the sensation of stubble against her palm, of an alien arm around her naked shoulders.

Smiling, she turned her head and kissed the hand cupping her naked shoulder in sleeping possession.

'My love,' said Annis softly.

CHAPTER EIGHT

ANNIS never liked Sunday mornings. Ever since the day she woke up to find that her mother had left after a loud Saturday night party she had equated Sundays with dangerous unpredictability. Anything could happen on a Sunday.

So if there was going to be a day on which she woke up in bed with the world's most fickle architect, it was going to be a Sunday. She opened her eyes.

Oh, no!

She had made love with a womaniser whose attention span was a maximum of a month! What was more, to crown it all, she was working for him! She had to be out of her mind! She shut her eyes again with a groan.

The trouble with shutting her eyes was that instantly she slipped back into awareness of her other senses: the softness of her flesh against his; the luxurious warmth of snuggling against him, like two animals in a burrow; the herbal scent of his cologne on her pillow, on *her*; the sheer bliss of utter relaxation.

Beside her Kosta stirred comfortably and hooked an arm round her. He did not open his eyes. But suddenly utter relaxation was no longer an option. Annis gritted her teeth and lay as still as a mouse, waiting for him to go to sleep so she could sort her head out.

Unpredictable as always, he did open his eyes then. His eyes were surprisingly alert.

'Something wrong?'

Annis smiled weakly. 'No.'

His arm tightened. 'Sure?'

'I—er—think I'll get a drink of water.'

She eased out of his embrace and swung her legs to the floor.

'Dehydrated,' he said professionally. 'Too much champagne last night.'

'Too much everything last night,' muttered Annis.

'What?'

She did not repeat it, rummaging for something to cover her. Nothing came to hand so she had to pad across to one of the cupboards to fetch a robe. Kosta plumped the pillow up behind his head and watched with deep appreciation. Annis could feel his lazy gaze on her nakedness and could have hit him.

How on earth did I get myself into this?

She extracted a kimono and pulled it round her, tugging at the embroidered silk as if it were a dish-rag. She was furious with herself, even more than with him. She had *known* he was a serial sensualist. Why hadn't she remembered it last night?

'Something *is* wrong.'

Annis deliberately misunderstood. Keeping her back to him she said, 'I'll be all right after I've had a drink of water.'

'Come here,' he said softly.

Oh, the temptation of it! Her body knew his now. Treacherously, it felt they belonged. Annis had to fight not to turn and rush back into all that warmth and delight.

But no woman in her right mind was going to let herself be trapped into belonging for a month, she thought grimly.

'Come *here*.'

'In a bit,' said Annis in a strangled voice.

She fled.

She drank her water but she did not go back to bed. Instead, she made herself some tea and took it into the sitting room. In their mad passion last night, she and Kosta had left all the table lamps glowing.

Annis flinched. She *never* left lights on. Even when she was catatonic with tiredness, she still had a ritual of tidying that left the room spick and span, waiting for her to start the new day tomorrow. Annis *relied* on that ritual. Now she looked at last night's disorder and felt as if she had walked into another dimension. As if she was no longer Annis Carew and her life had no more certainties in it.

All because of Kosta, who would stay a month if she was lucky. After which he would presumably move on to pastures new, leaving her—where? In the middle of the fifth dimension with no signposts.

What had he done to her? What had she let him do?

Berating herself thoroughly, Annis went through the room, turning off lights and plumping up cushions as if her life depended on it. Then she sank down on the armchair in the window and cradled the warm mug to her kimonoed breast. Bleak autumn winds were stirring the passion flower that climbed over her small balcony. Annis shivered.

The man was a sexual buccaneer. She had seen his little black book on his computer. Yet last night she had called him her love. Her only hope was that, having been carried away with the glory of the moment, she would find that she had not meant it this morning.

'What's cooking?' said Kosta behind her.

Three things happened simultaneously. Annis swung round, nearly dropping her mug and spilling tea far and wide. Kosta, incongruously alluring with a bath towel looped—just—over his narrow hips, gave her a sleepy, lopsided smile. And Annis realised that she had meant it all right. No matter how sensibly her left brain analysed the issues to prove otherwise, the truth was that she was in love with this renegade. Certainly hopelessly and probably unalterably. But, whichever way you dressed it up, horribly in love.

'Oh, *no!*'

She dropped her head in her hands. The mug fell to the floor unheeded. Kosta shot across the room and fell on one knee beside her chair.

'You've hurt yourself.'

Oh, boy, had she hurt herself! He could not begin to guess.

'No,' said Annis in a muffled voice.

'That stuff must have been hot.'

He took her in his arms. There was not enough bath towel between them. Annis could feel his skin, the amazing organic whole that was Kosta, under her hands. In spite of herself, she caught her breath at the wonder of it. If he had persuaded her, she would have done anything for him then, no matter how deep her doubts.

But he did not know about the doubts; he was much too sure of himself. 'You should stick to champagne in the mornings,' he said, a smile in his voice. 'That way you don't get scalded.'

For a heavenly moment Annis let herself lie against him. Her cheek lay against the warmth of a hair-ruffled chest. It even *felt* like love. She felt his hand move over her hair. She had to stop herself turning her head so she could kiss him just where his heart beat so steadily.

But then she reminded herself exactly *why* he was so sure of himself. And how many other women must have lain against him like this, basking briefly, so briefly, in the illusion of love. She folded her lips together so hard they hurt and flinched.

'You *did* burn yourself,' he said in concern. 'Show me.'

'No.' Annis pushed him away and scrabbled upright. 'You startled, me that's all.'

Her eyes felt suspiciously moist. She scrubbed her face with the back of her hand and tried not to sniff. Kosta loosened his hold on her but he did not let her go entirely. He sat back on his heels and scanned her face.

'What is it?'

If he had used one word of endearment, if he had even called her by her name, Annis would have told him every single doubt and fear she harboured. But he did not. She felt her heart contract with pain.

She stood up and stepped round him.

'Nothing,' she said in a much steadier voice. 'I need to get the tea out of the carpet before it stains.'

She came back with an armful of cloths and cleaning materials gathered at random from under the kitchen sink. Blankly she stared at the largest stain on the pale Chinese rug. She had blotted up spills over and over again since she first bought the impractical colour. This time she could not even remember what to do first.

Back in that fifth dimension where nothing normal held good any more, Annis thought grimly.

Aloud she said brightly, 'I need my cleaning lady. I haven't the faintest idea what to do.' Her voice was tight with tension

For some reason that made Kosta frown as none of her previous evasiveness had done. He took a dry cloth from her impatiently. Then he dropped it over the stain and stamped on it a couple of times. When he picked it up the mark had gone.

'Oh,' said Annis, feeling a fool. 'An expert.' And she gave a high pitched laugh.

'Inherited skill,' he said dryly.

'What?'

'It's in the blood. That was what my mother did. Clean people's houses.'

Annis was so unnerved her throat tightened even harder. As a result her voice came out in a high drawl 'Oh?'

He looked at her narrowly. 'Does it matter?'

Annis had the feeling that she was looking into a gigantic elephant trap.

'To me?' Still that horrible, high voice. She struggled to control it. 'No, why should it?'

He did not like that either. She saw it at once.

'Maybe because I matter.'

Was this another of his obscure warnings?

Annis said helplessly, 'I don't understand.'

He looked down at the cloth in his hand as if he did not know how it had come there.

'You mean, I don't matter to you?'

It sounded almost as if he wanted to matter, thought Annis. And this was the man who'd told her that commitment was strictly provisional. What did he *want*?

She said, 'Do you want to matter?'

She sounded horrible, she thought in despair, arch and so-phisticated and quite as if she did not care a jot.

At least that must have been what Kosta thought. His face stiffened.

'Don't play games with me, Annis.'

Her evil genius prompted her to say, 'You mean you're the only one allowed to play games?'

His face closed up completely. 'What does that mean?'

Annis was remembering Jamie: the neglect, the point-scoring, the misaligned assumptions. And the way she had always ended apologising. Jamie had been able to have one of their frozen arguments and then steam off to work and put it out of his mind. But she hadn't. It had nearly finished her career, to say nothing of her self-respect.

'I can't afford this,' she said from the heart.

The bones of his face stood out like a metal warrior-mask she had once seen in a museum. It made him look terrifying.

'Tell me one thing,' he said, barely opening his lips. 'What was last night about?'

Annis could not meet his eyes. 'I had too much to drink.'

'Not before you arrived. You threw yourself at me. You came dressed to throw yourself at me.'

Her eyes flew up, indignant. 'I *didn't.*'

But he took no notice. 'What was it? Revenge because I said you were no good at flirting?'

She was appalled 'Don't be stupid.'

'Or was it simpler than that? Was it an experiment? New look, new man for the night?'

It was so far from the truth that Annis laughed aloud. It was a mistake.

Kosta looked at her for a long, unreadable moment. Except that he was not unreadable if you knew him, of course. Annis could feel the anger licking up behind the still face as if she was actually watching the thermometer rise.

Then he said quite pleasantly, 'How many men have you tied up in knots while you decided whether they were what you wanted?'

'*What?*'

'And I said you didn't know anything about chemistry,' he said reflectively. 'That must have given you a real laugh.'

'What do you mean?'

'That bedroom.' He jerked his head. 'When I saw it last

night I thought you were a secret sensualist—all that light and colour and texture when you keep everything out here so neutral it disappears. But I was wrong. It's your personal statement, isn't it?'

Annis was uneasy. 'I—I suppose so.'

'Your private joke against the rest of the world. Very inventive.' It was not a compliment. 'And I agree—,' savagery licked through the meditative tone '—you're right to keep it behind a closed door. Gives a man the illusion of having made a discovery.'

Annis blenched. 'No,' she protested faintly.

'And when he thinks he has, you head for the hills.'

'I don't. I didn't—'

But she had bolted for privacy this morning and they both knew it.

He came up to her and looked down into her face as if he was examining it under a microscope.

'So what happened? Night of passion not up to your expectations?'

Her eyes flared. He stopped dead and Annis saw comprehension leap into his face.

'No, of course it isn't that,' he said, as if discovering the answer to an intellectual puzzle. 'You weren't expecting a night of passion at all, were you?'

'I—'

'And it's scared you silly.'

Annis began to feel sick. 'Of course not,' she said loudly. *'Why?'*

'It did not scare me. Nothing scares me.'

He ignored that. 'Passion not on your agenda, lovely Annis? Too red-blooded for you, is it?'

Annis saw that he was very angry. She had to stop that hard, angry voice.

'Stop it,' she said clearly.

He did not seem to hear her. He certainly wasn't listening.

'Bit too close to real life for a millionaire's daughter who doesn't know how to clean her own carpets?'

He was still holding the cloth. With a vicious overarm

movement he suddenly flung it against the wall. It recoiled hard. Annis jumped.

He turned a smile on her that was all teeth and fury. 'A shock was it, last night?'

Annis lifted her chin. 'For both of us, by the sound of it.'

'It got out of control, didn't it? You didn't like that.' His flashing smile cut like a knife. 'Doesn't go with the cool image. Nor with all the things you don't do.'

'If you say one word about my not dating, I shall throw things,' said Annis dangerously.

Kosta grabbed her by the upper arms. 'No, you won't, you'll listen…'

Annis gave a yell of indignation and kicked out.

Kosta stopped dead.

'What am I doing?' he said hardly above a whisper.

None of her kicks had connected but he let her go as if she were radioactive.

'Out of control, indeed,' he said quietly. He was very pale. 'You're right. This is nasty. I'll go.'

Annis sank bonelessly onto the sofa. She had not stopped trembling when he came back into the sitting room, fully dressed. At least he was wearing his dress trousers and last night's crumpled white shirt. He had the black jacket looped over his shoulder.

She pressed quivering fingers to her mouth. She felt as if she had just fallen out of a rocket and was still falling, not sure that she was ever going to hit the ground. It made her feel sick.

Kosta did not look much better. Maybe it was the night's growth of beard that made him look exhausted, Annis thought. But that did not account for the bleakness in his eyes.

'Goodbye,' he said formally. 'It's been an education.'

She could not bear him to leave her trembling on the sofa like a fool. She got to her feet without knowing quite how she managed it. She plastered on the smile she had learned after her mother had run away, the one she'd used when she'd said to kind mothers of her school friends that, yes, she had had a wonderful time, and thank you for inviting her to the party, but she just felt a bit sick and wanted to go home now.

'You're welcome,' said Annis brightly and, as it turned out, lethally.

He spun round, his anger leaping out at her. Annis quailed at the blaze in his eyes. He threw his jacket aside and strode across to her.

It was less a kiss than a brand on her mouth. His unshaven skin grazed her. But worse, far worse, was the pain when he let her go and she saw the contempt in his eyes.

She dragged the back of her hand across her mouth. She did not know who she hated more—Kosta or herself.

As if he could read her mind, he said mockingly, 'And I thought I was your love?'

For a moment Annis did not understand him. Then she realised. She had thought he was asleep. But he had not been. He had been secretly awake—and listening! It felt like the ultimate betrayal. For a moment she was so shocked by the pain she literally stopped breathing.

Then her heart slammed back into action. Oh, of course he had not been asleep. He had been pretending. As her father had said, as she had seen herself, Kosta liked to win. *Had* to win.

She said between frozen lips, 'Is there anything you won't do to score a point?'

He was smiling, though the smile didn't seem to reach his eyes.

'That wasn't a point,' he drawled, his accent pronounced. 'That was total victory.'

Annis would not have believed it possible to hurt so much and still be on her feet. She tortured her mouth into a smile, trying to look as if she did not care. But she not think it deceived Kosta for a moment.

'That was quite a journey you took me on last night,' he mused. 'I hope it got you what you wanted.'

'No, you don't,' said Annis, made literal by shock. She blinked tears away and kept smiling, as she had learned to do over the years at Lynda's parties. It felt grotesque.

'Oh, I don't know,' he said softly, as if he were considering an academic question. 'I got what I wanted, after all. It's only fair that you should do the same.'

This was a nightmare.

'Thank you,' said Annis politely.

'But once is enough. I don't think either of us has behaved too well. So forgive me if I don't want to repeat the experience.'

Even years of practice could not keep the horrible smile in place. Annis was appalled and it showed. Her hand went to her mouth, in horror. Stricken tears sprang unstoppably.

Only Kosta did not see them. The front door was already banging behind him.

It was a bad few hours but eventually Annis pulled herself together. Not entirely together, of course, that would have been too much to ask. But sufficiently together to strip and remake the bed, wash everything in her room that wasn't nailed down and spring clean the flat, including a full shampoo of the unstained rugs.

Eventually she sat down at her computer and went determinedly through her schedule of work in progress. By that time she only had to stop to blow her nose or blot the damp bits under her eyes every ten minutes or so. Her ribs hurt from suppressing heaving sobs. But at least she could see the screen without blinking tears away.

The telephone rang. Annis tensed.

It's him. It has to be him. I don't want to talk to him.

I have to talk to him. I don't know what to say.

She picked up the phone and said her number breathlessly.

'Annis? Is that you? Have you got a cold or something?'

'Bella.' The anticlimax was almost painful.

'How are you today? Got over seeing Jamie?'

Jamie? Annis gave a hollow laugh.

'Yes, I think I'm over that one, thank you.'

'I just wish I knew how to do that. You are so in control of your life.'

'I wouldn't bet on it,' muttered Annis.

'I just keep making a complete prat of myself,' Bella steamed on, not hearing. 'I can't seem to stop putting my foot in it.'

Annis sighed. But she loved Bella and she knew a cry for help when she heard one. Besides, looking at her work schedule on the screen, she was beginning to get panicky about the number of days she still had to go to the offices of Vitale and Partners. It might prove therapeutic to stop picking over her own disaster and start looking at someone else's. Anyway, it would be a distraction.

'Do you want to come over for supper?' she asked.

Bella, when she arrived, was more subdued than Annis had ever known her. She wandered round the kitchen while Annis simmered pasta and shredded ham.

'Mother says don't give up hope. But I don't see how I can do anything else.'

Bella leaned on the counter and sliced transparent slivers of Parmesan off the big block that Annis had brought back from her last holiday in Tuscany. She nibbled a flake of it thoughtfully.

'I mean, I've tried everything. Outrageous party girl. Kid next door. Sober citizen.'

'Sober citizen?' In spite of her miseries, Annis choked with laughter at the picture this conjured up.

Bella twinkled. 'Well, computer-clone chic, I suppose you'd call it. Sensible shoes and a cardigan.'

'I'd call it playing dress up,' said Annis astringently. She drained the pasta and turned her attention to the carbonara sauce. 'Could it possibly be that this man had seen you in your—er—more unzipped moments and suspected he was being set up?'

'No,' said Bella despondently. 'He didn't notice me in my more unzipped moments.'

'Every man notices you in your more unzipped moments,' Annis assured her.

Bella was without false modesty. 'I know. He doesn't. He spent more time talking to Tony.'

'Dad?' Annis looked up from the sauce, briefly alarmed.

'Bella, you haven't fallen for some widget fancier at Dad's company, have you? Most of those guys are married, for heaven's sake. It would be terribly unfair both to him and to Dad if you—'

'He's not a widget fancier,' said Bella hastily. 'He doesn't work for Dad. Well, not really. And he's certainly not married.'

Annis took the sauce off the gas.

'Well, that's all right, then.'

'Only because he's too fast on his feet,' said Bella gloomily.

Annis was pouring the sauce over the pasta but she paused for a startled millisecond. A crazy idea occurred to her.

'Who are we talking about, Isabella?' she asked quietly.

But Bella was carrying the salad to the table and pretended not to hear. She continued to turn a deaf ear to every demand for the unknown sex object's name throughout the meal. She did, however, explain very fully his attraction, his powers of evasion and his exceptional indifference to herself.

'I mean—if every man in the room is looking at me and he is looking at his watch, what's the point?'

Annis knew by now that Bella was not going to tell her his name. Of course it was absolutely out of the question that Bella would have fallen for Kosta. She and Bella were never attracted to the same man. Besides, if Kosta, the connoisseur, had seen a dish like Bella on offer, he would never have spared a glance on Annis.

Even so—'How old is he?' she asked cunningly.

'Another adult like me.'

'Do I know him?'

Bella gave her an odd, defiant look. She seemed almost ashamed. 'You've had the treatment, same as I did. Only you're too sensible to let it get to you.'

No, of course it couldn't be Kosta, thought Annis. Bella would not be so defiant if it were Kosta. Every woman in his office, every woman at Lynda's dinner party and probably every woman in the world seemed to agree that he was the sexiest thing on two legs. Bella, a connoisseur herself in this area, would not be ashamed of telling if she had developed a crush on Konstantin Vitale.

Unseen, Annis heaved a sigh of relief. She did not think she could bear it if she and Bella were falling apart over the same heart breaker. Tragedy was one thing, she told herself, farce would be much harder to endure with any dignity. It just showed how shaken up she was that she had even let it cross her mind. It was clearly ridiculous.

Meantime she had to get through work on Monday with a furious Kosta in residence.

But she had reckoned without his lightning changes of plan.

Kosta was flying out to Milan, Tracy told her sunnily. Nobody had seen him, though he had left copious instructions for everyone. He had simply come to the office, swept up his papers and gone before even Annis could be expected to arrive on the premises.

'Haven't had a row with him, have you?' asked Tracy, laughing heartily at her own joke.

Annis smiled weakly. Then rallied. 'He shouldn't have left you anything except his emergency number if the delegation programme is working,' she said firmly. 'Bring me his list of instructions. Then call a meeting of everyone for eleven. We've got to get this sorted out once and for all.'

As she'd suspected, the list was random and full of minutiae that he should not have been bothered with. And he still had not remembered about the leaking roof.

'Right,' said Annis grimly to the assembled staff. 'I'm going to go round each of you and I want you to tell me what you think are your five most important things to do this morning. This is not a test. This is just to see what we agree on before we decide what to do.'

They looked at each other. 'But Kosta—'

Annis snapped. 'Forget Kosta. Just like he's forgotten you. This is about making this place *work*. He can swan around in Milan until he's blue in the face. When he comes back, you're going to be on top of the work flow or I, personally, will put the lot of you through the shredder.'

*   *   *

But Kosta was not swanning around in Milan. He breezed into the Milan office of Vitale and Partners for an interval only marginally longer than he had spent in the London premises that morning. Then he picked up a rental car that looked as if it would be happier on the racetrack than the *autostrada* and set its nose to the south. He was driving very fast.

He had lost his cool with Annis. He could not remember the last time that had happened. He considered the point savagely. Eventually he came to the conclusion, somewhere north of Genoa, that it had never happened before. Not like that. Not so completely that he had almost been betrayed into laying hands on a woman and shaking some sense into her. He still recoiled at the thought. That made him even more furious with Annis.

The worst of it was that, for the first time in his life, he did not know what to do next. He, Konstantin Vitale, architectural visionary, international sophisticate and all round brilliant brain, had not the slightest idea what to do about a woman. Not even one of the glamorous social princesses that he normally hung out with, either. Just an ordinary woman with a career and a family and bad taste in boyfriends.

Only she wasn't ordinary. He had known it from the moment he'd looked up and seen her across her stepmother's drawing room. Known it when she'd announced that she did not date and had looked at him as if she'd expected that to deter him.

A smile—the first in hours, it seemed—invaded his eyes.

She might know everything there was to know about business management, his Annis, but she sure had not got a handle on human nature yet.

His Annis. That was the crux of it. Why didn't she realise it?

But he knew the answer to that too. It was that damned lack of self-respect again. Now that he was calmer, he could just imagine what she thought had happened at the dance. His smile died.

Annis would think that she had been too upset about that creep to know what she was doing. So she'd had too much to drink. And then, as she would see it, wicked, predatory Kosta had waltzed her into bed before she'd had time to think.

He shifted sharply in the low sports-car seat. Well, there was a grain of truth there.

She had driven him half mad that evening, dressed like a temptress and flirting with every man in sight. He had known she was too unpractised to know the effect that her sweet, dangerous challenge was having on him. But by the end he just hadn't cared. He had wanted her from the first moment he'd seen her, though she'd refused to recognise it. That night it had seemed that a path had opened up to take him straight to the heart of his desire.

But to Annis it would look simpler. And a whole lot nastier. She would perceive a serial womaniser who'd seen his chance and had taken it.

Kosta banged his fist on the dashboard so hard that the CD player jumped track, which was supposed to be impossible.

And that was why she had suddenly turned into the millionaire's daughter in the morning, all high drawling voice and pretend indifference. Because it had been pretend. He knew that now. He would have known it then, if she hadn't managed to get him on the raw.

And, being hurt, he had struck back. Harder than Annis knew how. He could still see the stricken look on her face. Though she had fought back, his Annis. She would always fight back.

Hell, he'd been watching her like a private detective for days. He knew how hard she fought the moment anyone seemed to threaten her self-control. He probably knew more about her responses than she did herself.

I know she kisses like an angel, thought Kosta involuntarily. *And when she's half-awake she burrows against you as if you're her rock. I know she seems surprised by her own sensuality. She thinks she's so cool and logical but her responses give her away.*

The car shot forward, increasing to a speed that the manufacturers would probably have said was impossible. Kosta eased his foot off the accelerator, muttering a curse. He eased his collar.

What had happened to him? He was an accomplished driver. He never took his emotions out on his car. Never.

Kosta clenched the sports-car steering wheel so hard he almost snapped it. Emotions? For an uptight, nasty-tongued, spoilt daughter of a rich industrialist? She was everything he despised, everything that his mother had struggled against to get him an education. Everything he had mocked and avoided all his life. He could not care for her. Even if she did kiss like an angel.

But then he remembered the way she'd flinched when he'd said that passion scared her. And—worse—the look on her face when he'd flung at her, 'And I thought I was your love?'

Oh he had struck a nerve there, all right. He had been too angry to realise it at the time. But that was when he had really struck home. And he wished from his heart that he could undo it. He could not bear to think of his Annis hurt as he had hurt her.

Kosta unclenched his hands from the wheel and drew a long breath. Quite suddenly it was all perfectly clear. She *was* his Annis. He just had to get her to believe it.

He looked across the wide plain. The church tower of a little hilltop village was outlined against the grey sky. He smiled.

'Well, there's one way to do that,' he said aloud. 'And it had better be *soon*.'

CHAPTER NINE

'Two messages for you,' said Tracy.

She pushed a scrubby piece of paper under Annis's nose. Annis looked up from Kosta's desk and sighed. She had been meaning to get round to doing something about formalising the message taking. But in the ten days since Kosta had taken off she had been too busy. She made a note on her memory pad.

'Thank you.'

Tracy did not go. Annis looked up again.

'What is it?'

'Do you want me to book the flights?'

'What?' Annis looked at the messages. Her heart seemed to stop. Then it started to thump like a steam hammer. 'Oh, I see.'

One was from Roy, reporting back from a meeting with Gil de la Court. The other was from Vitale's Milan office. That was what had started the hammer going. She was required to go to San Giorgio at once. Annis looked quickly at Tracy but the girl did not seem to be unduly interested. She was just waiting to see if she needed to get on to the travel agent.

Annis cleared her throat and hoped that her heart did not sound as loud to Tracy as it did to her. 'Where is San Giorgio?'

'It's a castle in the south of Italy somewhere. Kosta goes there to work when he doesn't want to be interrupted.'

'Oh,' said Annis hollowly.

But Tracy was still mercifully uninterested.

''Course, he's not there at the moment. He's in Milan. I suppose he wants you to review his systems there.'

There was a small pause.

'Yes,' said Annis at last in a flat tone. 'Yes, that will be it, of course.'

'So do you want me to get the flights?' asked Tracy patiently. 'It takes a bit of doing. Kosta always takes a helicopter from Naples.'

Annis was shocked. 'I can't do that. The expense!'

Tracy shrugged. 'It's a sort of taxi service, I think. We run an account, anyway. I'll just charge it to the partnership.'

Annis debated. 'Well, check it with Milan,' she decided. 'If it's really necessary, I suppose it's up to Vitale's to get me there.'

'Okey-doke,' said Tracy casually. 'And what about the other message?'

'I'll deal with that.'

She picked up the phone and Tracy left.

It was just as well for Annis's peace of mind that she did not see Tracy break into a little dance once she had closed the door behind her.

The other message was more encouraging. Gil de la Court, having wavered for months, now wanted them to start work as soon as possible.

'I told him we'd do our best but no promises. Can you finish up there by the end of the week?' said Roy.

'No. Maybe next week,' offered Annis. 'You start and I'll join you as soon as I can get away.'

He had to be content with that.

She got to Naples without incident. There, the helicopter looked solid enough. Annis tucked her briefcase-cum-overnight bag behind her legs and tried to look as if she flew in helicopters to unknown destinations every day of the week. But she nearly lost her cool when she saw San Giorgio.

Tracy had called it a castle. It looked like a hilltop fortress. From the circling helicopter it looked about as isolated and forbidding as you could get. Far below it, waves crashed onto a deserted crescent of beach. Black uneven steps could be seen, cut into the rock face that led down to the shore with its rudimentary landing stage. There was no road that she could see and not so much as a shepherd's hut in the wild, rock-strewn hills below her. Annis thought she had never seen a place so desolate in her life.

The helicopter set down gently on an apron that seemed to jut perilously over the edge of the cliff. The pilot gave her a beaming smile. Presumably relieved that he hadn't actually flown the thing into the rock face, thought Annis. She gave him a congratulatory nod and fished for her belongings.

When she sat up straight, the door had been swung open and she came nose to nose with Kosta.

'Oh, help,' said Annis in pure reflex.

The noise of the helicopter drowned her voice but he must have read her lips. He grinned. His hair was blowing all over the place and rain—or was it spray from the wild sea below?—had plastered his denim shirt to his body. Annis felt her hands go clammy.

He grabbed her bag and her hand and towed her towards the castle. The pilot did not even turn off the ailerons. He just checked the door closure, raised a hand and was off.

Kosta opened a weathered oak door and tugged Annis inside. In the distance the fusillade of helicopter engine died away. Annis became aware of total silence. A nasty suspicion occurred to her.

'Is there anyone else here?'

'Only the ghosts.'

Annis had recovered her poise. She looked at him with dislike. 'You're not funny.'

He was leading the way up a spiral staircase. It wound round a stone pillar that looked as old as the world. Their feet clattered eerily on the worn stone steps.

Kosta looked back over his shoulder and his eyes glinted. They were as green as a cat's. No mistaking it, thought Annis indignantly, he was enjoying himself.

'Not trying to be funny. We've got plenty of ghosts. Greeks. Romans. Normans who built the castle. Arab raiders who sacked it. And then the brigands moved in.'

Annis could not help herself. She shuddered and looked round quickly. It was pure instinct and she could have kicked herself the moment she did it. Especially when he laughed softly.

'Don't worry about it. I'll keep you safe from brigands.'

It was that dark treacle caressing voice, the one that he used to charm the birds out of the trees, the one that had first turned her against him. Oh, how right she had been to distrust him on sight! Annis stopped dead and tipped her head back to look up at him defiantly.

'I can keep myself safe, thank you. What are you up to, Kosta? What am I doing here?'

'You know what you're doing here. Helping me sort out my life.'

Annis narrowed her eyes suspiciously. 'What does that mean?'

'Just that you were right. I need you.'

The staircase was full of shadows. She could not tell whether he was laughing or deadly serious. She did not know which frightened her more.

It was crazy, of course. She was a modern woman. She was independent and self-possessed and she had proved her competence. She was not frightened of anyone. At least not as long as they followed ordinary rules of reasonable behaviour.

So of course she was not afraid of Kosta. Kosta was a civilised man. Well, most of the time.

Annis suddenly remembered a couple of occasions when his claim to civilisation had been a bit rocky. Her heart contracted treacherously. But not with fear.

She said abruptly, '*Are* we here alone?'

He smiled down at her. 'What do you think?'

'I think,' she said slowly, 'that you would do almost anything to get your own way.'

The green eyes flickered oddly. 'Does that scare you?'

'No,' said Annis. She found it was true. She shook back her hair and smiled up at him with sudden brilliance. 'No, I'm not scared.'

He did not say anything. But he gave a long, long sigh, as if he had been climbing an ice wall and had unexpectedly reached the top.

He took her into a huge kitchen, with smoke-blackened beams and a fireplace several tall men could have stood up in. Comprehensive twenty-first century kitchen equipment took up a tiny corner of it. A brigade could have eaten at the refectory table.

Their footsteps echoed on the medieval flags. If Annis had wanted confirmation that there was no one else but the two of them in the castle, that deserted and echoing kitchen would have done it.

'Why?' she said.

He did not pretend to misunderstand her. 'I gave the staff a long weekend. I thought you and I could do with some time together—and the space in which to spend it.'

Annis looked round the vast room. 'Well, we've certainly got that.'

Then she heard what she had said. *We.* As if they were a couple; partners; acknowledged lovers. She had never said *we* before. Not aloud. Not even in her head, maybe. She felt as if she had taken some huge step over a chasm, without even realising it was there.

'Don't look so worried,' Kosta said softly.

Reading her mind again! Annis's eyes flew to his in shock. He smiled. 'It will be all right. I promise.'

Annis drew a little breath that was half a sob. All right, she was not afraid of Kosta. But herself? Total honesty, she decided bravely, was the only way.

'I'm out of my depth here,' she said bluntly. 'Don't forget I'm no good at flirting.'

'I'm counting on it.'

'Oh.'

Kosta's lips twitched. If she had looked at him, Annis would have seen his face was full of amused tenderness. But she did not. She was too busy trying to keep her balance.

After a moment he said briskly, 'I won't take you on the

guided tour yet. But the kitchen is the root of the castle. If you get lost, come back here. Not least because there is a map on the wall. Come here.'

She went and stood beside him. The floor plans looked like the architectural drawings she had been used to seeing round Vitale's office.

'You've rebuilt the place,' she said in sudden understanding.

'It's not finished yet. Look, you can see. The stuff that's outlined in blue is completed. The rest will get done over time.'

The floor plans looked astonishingly complicated, with little half-landings and odd rooms that did not seem to fit in anywhere. She said so.

'That's because the castle is built into the rock. Some of the rooms are not much more than hollowed-out caves. It was amazing what they managed to do with primitive tools.'

'Primitive,' echoed Annis.

She would never have imagined ultra-sophisticated, urban Kosta relishing anything primitive. And yet here he was in this medieval space looking as if he belonged here, savouring the achievements of the construction engineers of the Middle Ages.

A faint expression of annoyance crossed his face. 'I'm not just brocade jackets and champagne, you know.'

Annis shivered. 'You've got to stop reading my mind like that.'

The annoyance died. He looked at her, arrested. 'Was I?'

But Annis had been betrayed into one admission. She was not going to compound the error. She turned away and concentrated on the map.

'Where am I sleeping?'

'In my arms.'

She was tracing a crazily fractured corridor. 'I'll never find my way—*what*?'

He was so close she could feel the heat of his body but he did not touch her. Annis held herself very still and did not turn to face him. She was almost certain that he was bending over her, drinking in the scent of her hair. Her heart lurched and began to thunder.

He said quietly, 'You will sleep with me.'

She did turn then. And saw he was deadly serious. He was rather pale under his tan and the green eyes were no longer laughing.

She said explosively, 'You're not serious. You can't just announce something like that. What if I don't want to?'

'Don't you?'

She ignored that. 'What if I refuse to?'

He did not answer for a moment. When he did, she had the feeling that he was groping his way through a landscape he had never visited before. And that he was trying to tell the exact truth. It was so unexpected that she heard him out in silence. Simmering silence. But at least she let him finish.

'Annis, you and I bring out the worst in each other sometimes. But there's something there and it's not over.'

He paused. She said nothing.

'When you and I made love—well, neither of was using our heads, were we?'

She snorted derisively but she did not interrupt.

'I knew it was too soon for both of us. You'd made me mad. And then you—well, to be honest you drove me crazy. I had to have you. You must know that. And it wasn't just me, either, was it? You were as desperate as I was.'

The look he gave her challenged her to admit it. Annis shrugged, looking away.

'The moment I got into that fantasy room of yours, I knew it was a mistake. You felt invaded. I saw that. And I—well, I suddenly realised how much there was about you I didn't know. But, like I said, it wasn't exactly our brains giving the orders.'

Annis swallowed. 'No,' she muttered at last.

Her skin, her very blood, felt sensitised to his every move, his breath even. But Kosta did not touch her.

'So I thought if you came here—to my private special

place—you would feel different. You would know as much about me as I do now about you.' He smiled suddenly. 'Hell, you'll probably end up knowing everything there is to know about me.'

She did not speak. She could not.

'I thought, if I let you see me here, you would not feel so vulnerable.'

Vulnerable? She felt naked!

He said quietly, 'Sleep with me, Annis.'

Her head whirled. She said nothing.

He made a quick movement, as if he would have taken her into his arms then. But she flinched and he thrust his hands into his pockets.

'We don't need to make love if you don't want to. We won't do anything you don't want to. Just let me hold you.' The green eyes were serious. 'I know you're afraid of being out of control. But trust me this once and I won't ever ask you to take such a gamble again.'

Annis swallowed. This time she could see the chasm ahead and it terrified her. Couldn't he see that? Why didn't he take her in his arms?

But Kosta was keeping a meticulous distance. His mouth was drawn.

'How can I get you to stop fighting me?' A note almost of despair had invaded his voice. No seducer's mellifluous tones now. Just a man desperately in earnest who did not know what to say or do next. 'Annis, this thing we've got—it happens once in a lifetime. Give it a chance. Please.'

She looked into the handsome Byronic face and saw honesty. It terrified her. At the same time it made her feel as if she had been given the world.

'I—don't know.' Her voice sounded strange to her.

His eyes were suddenly alert. 'Look—stay close to me today. I'll take you round the castle. You can reorganise my plans if you like. Then this evening we'll cook a meal together. I'll make a fire; we can read or watch television or talk. Let's just be like an old married couple today. See how it feels.

Then, if you still want to sleep alone, you can. If you want to leave you can and I won't say a word to stop you. But give me today.'

It was his negotiating mode, infinitely reasonable, wholly unthreatening. But the chasm was still there and none of his calm practicalities could hide it. Would he get her across or let her fall? If she did fall, her self-respect would be ripped to shreds. Worse, her heart would shatter.

Because Annis knew, without any question at all, that Konstantin Vitale had the power to break her heart now. Could she risk it? Could she afford not to risk it?

She looked up and saw his expression. It was almost unrecognisable, so level, so tender. He put a hand out to her. Without even knowing she was doing it, Annis took it.

The hours that followed were strange, almost dreamlike. An almighty storm blew up. The afternoon went dark. Thunder rolled making the lights flicker.

Kosta showed her the great hall, hung with tapestries that wafted in the constant draughts and talked of Calabrian history.

'It was one of the great colonies of Greece. There are still remains to be found. But we have earthquakes and it has been inaccessible so long. Archaeologists find other places more attractive. There is a bridge across the gorge to the village and they think they have found an old road there. I've been asked if I'll allow a dig next summer.'

'And will you?'

'Of course.'

'Although they'll invade your privacy? You did say this is your private place.'

'No place is that private. I've told you, I don't believe in ownership.'

Annis fingered the tapestry. It was seventeenth century and threadbare in places. It must have cost him a fortune. Just as the high-tech appliances lost in the vaulted kitchen downstairs must have. He was not just camping here. He was making it habitable—more, he was making it beautiful—as if he believed he owned it. She said so.

His brows twitched together in a quick frown. 'Clever.' He sounded irritated.

'No. Just intrigued. There seems to be a flaw in your argument somewhere.'

'Nobody else wanted it,' he said, goaded. 'It was falling apart.'

'So why were you the one to come to the rescue?'

He frowned even harder. Then gave a quick dismissive shrug. 'My father came from round here originally. I was sixteen and looking for my roots.'

'Oh.'

Annis digested this. He was looking forbidding, as if he wanted to end the subject there. But he had invited her to see him as deeply as he had seen her and she wanted to know.

'Do you still see your father?'

For a moment she thought he would not answer. Then he said, 'I suppose I asked for this. Yes, I see him. You want to know all about it, I suppose?'

Annis nodded.

'He came from Calabria, one of the hill villages further north. He went to Croatia, had a holiday fling with my mother, moved on to the States. She always thought he was a great aristocrat but he wasn't—just the son of a rural land owner with a good line in self promotion.'

It sounded bitter. He brooded.

Annis said, 'Do you dislike him?'

Kosta came out of his brown study. 'What? No, of course not. What happened is history, and not my history, at that. He didn't know about me until both he and my mother had married other people and had children of their own. He was kind enough when I went to the States. We're not close.'

'And your mother?'

'We're not close either, but for other reasons. She's always treated me as if I was some heir to a foreign kingdom. That's why she went to Australia: looking for education and a better life because I was a sort of sacred trust.' He scowled. 'Quite mad. Otherwise, she's a sensible woman, a very good mother to my stepbrothers. It was just me she thought was too important. I always felt like a cuckoo in the nest. Frankly it was a relief to everyone when I took to the road.'

Annis was having a revelation. 'So San Giorgio is the first home you have ever owned?'

'I've told you, I don't *own* places,' he said on a flash of temper.

'All right.' Annis was equable. 'The first place where you belonged.'

Kosta looked thunderstruck. Annis bit back a smile.

Later he walked her along the ramparts. The sky was ink-black but the sheet of rain had moved south.

'Look,' said Annis, 'a rainbow.'

It arced over the gun-metal sea like the entrance to paradise.

The wind blew her hair back from her face. It left her scar cruelly exposed. Instinctively she put up a hand to hide it.

'Don't,' Kosta said fiercely. He caught her hand and turned her to face him. 'Don't hide anything from me, good or bad.'

So Annis told him what she hardly even let herself remember. 'My mother said it was gross. That it ruined me. That was why she left my father. Because she couldn't bear to look at me.'

'Nonsense.'

'What?' Annis was not sure she had heard correctly.

Kosta bent towards her, shielding her from the wind so she could hear him distinctly. 'People leave their partners because something has gone wrong between them.'

Annis stared.

'Did she tell you she left because you were scarred?'

'I never saw her again.'

'OK, did your father tell you that?'

'No. But I knew.' Annis wrestled with unwelcome memory. 'I heard her say she couldn't bear to look at me.'

He kissed the scar very gently. 'She was probably in shock. I bet that was just after it happened.'

'Yes, it was,' admitted Annis.

'Not kind. Or sensible. But I'll bet she wasn't thinking of it as grounds for divorce. That was because there was something wrong between her and your father.'

Annis found, astonishingly, that she believed him. He put an arm round her and pulled her against his shoulder. It felt like a rock. She looked at the rainbow through an inexplicable mist before blinking it away. But she left her head on his shoulder trustfully.

Before he'd sent his staff away Kosta had made sure that the larder was well-stocked. Annis was no cook but she did not need to be. Kosta had her chopping green peppers and aubergines while he made a sauce for the pasta which was pure magic. They ate in the kitchen until the storm returned. Eventually there was a loud crash and all the lights went out, including the pilot light on the cooker.

'Just as well I lit a fire,' said Kosta, unmoved.

He lit some candles and set a tray with a couple of tiny glasses, a bottle full of something that looked like liquid lemon curd and a flat circular cake.

'Signora Sfogliatelle will provide the dessert.'

'Who is Signora Sfogliatelle?' asked Annis, trying not to wince as lightning forked across the sky beyond the windows.

He tapped the cake. 'Local speciality. Well, fairly local. Tastes of orange flowers. I've never had anything like it anywhere else in the world. Come on, we'll finish supper in front of the fire.'

He took her up another of those corkscrew stone staircases. This time the room was circular and small enough for the enormous fire to warm it deliciously. Annis saw a sheepskin rug, books and a large, battered chair with a brass Arabic table beside it. Beyond the firelight there were flickering shadows of dark furniture and more tapestries. High up, the walls were studded with tiny arrow slits through which the lightning was still visible.

Annis kicked off her shoes and sank down onto the rug. The neat skirt she had travelled in slid disreputably up her thighs. She did not care. She wiggled her toes luxuriously in the silky wool. Kosta put the tray down on the small table.

'You cut the cake. I'll open the *limoncello*.'

As Annis sliced into it, a scent of oranges and aromatic leaves vied with the wood smoke.

'Powerful,' she said, her nose twitching appreciatively.

Kosta was twisting the top off the bottle. He smiled down at her. 'Yes, I thought you'd like that, little sensualist that you are. And what about this?' He held the open bottle out to her.

Annis sniffed cautiously. The smell of lemon peel was so astringent it made her eyes water.

'Wow.'

'You drink it to get rid of a cold. Kills all known germs. But tonight, we're going to pour it over *la sfogliatelle*.' He did so and handed her a plate. 'Taste that.'

The taste filled her mouth with fiery citrus. She blinked.

'Very—energising,' said Annis truthfully.

She thought he would sit in the leather chair. It was clearly a favourite. But he did not. He slid down on the rug beside her.

'Is it?'

She turned her head and was looking straight into his eyes. They were so close, so intent, that her head swam.

'I—'

He took the plate away from her and put it up on the table.

'Out of harm's way,' he said, a smile in his voice.

The fire was making Annis feel voluptuously languid. But her instincts were all on tiptoe alert. She sat very straight and curled her legs to one side to give him more room.

'Kosta—'

He slid further down and touched an experimental finger to the hollow of her knee. She gave a gasp, half-surprise, half-pleasure. He looked up.

'You like that?'

Annis swallowed. 'I'm not sure.' Which was true.

'OK. More research needed.'

He stretched out along the rug and began to play his fingers along her skin as if she were a keyboard. He teased her foot, then her ankle, the sensitive place behind her knee. Annis wriggled, smiling. Sitting up straight was becoming more and more of an effort. Not a very rewarding effort. She felt her senses uncurl at that controlled, expert touch.

The playful, purposeful fingers moved higher. And suddenly she was not smiling any more. She stilled his hand.

He was undisturbed. 'Still not sure?' She could hear the smile in his voice.

He put his hands either side of her waist and pulled her down beside him. The smart business skirt concertinaed under her.

'That looks uncomfortable,' he said, and removed it.

She shivered, half-longing, half-reluctant. But she did not try to put the skirt on again. She lay still, looking at him very steadily.

Kosta put a possessive hand on her hip-bone. She knew it was possessive. She felt the claim he was staking as clearly as if he had said it aloud. He was, Annis was relieved to see, no longer undisturbed.

He said with difficulty, 'I said we wouldn't do anything you didn't want. You'd better tell me what you want before I—'

In the shadows his face was all cheekbones and dark hollows, tense with need. Annis looked away. In the hearth, flames wavered and danced mesmerisingly. The red core of the fire held little blue-green flames. She looked back quickly and saw they were reflected in his eyes. *As they must be in mine,* thought Annis.

For a moment she froze. Astonished at her own courage, she thought, *so here I go, then.*

Not taking her eyes from his face, she undid her sober cream silk blouse and let it fall away. It was a gesture of total surrender. Total trust.

Kosta made a ragged, disbelieving sound. Clumsy with haste, he stripped her of her remaining garments. As he tossed them aside, Annis thought how fragile they seemed. And how strong she felt without them. Strong and elemental.

He bent over her, as if she were some precious prize, and kissed her everywhere. Slowly, though he shook with his own need.

His exquisite courtesy moved her to tears, even while it had her reaching for him in hunger. When he finally slid inside her, she gave a little gasp of utter, astonished completeness.

Then the elemental took over.

At some point he stood up and threw more logs on the fire. As the sparks flew she watched avidly. In the firelight, he was lean and golden. *And mine,* thought Annis. Stretching up, she ran a lazy hand over his naked thigh and felt him quiver in response. He turned. *I did that,* she thought. She laughed up at him, triumphant in her new trust.

'So what was that about sleeping in your arms?' she teased.

'Soon,' he promised huskily.

But they did not sleep for hours.

Later he made up the fire for one last time and carried her into the shadows. The shadowed furniture turned out to be a bed, huge and comfortable and warm as an animal's burrow. But even so she did not sleep. She just lay in his arms in a daze of delighted senses and satisfied heart.

I have never been so happy. Did she say it aloud?

Kosta held her to his chest where his heart beat so strongly. He was playing with the hair on her neck.

'This time I'll say it,' he said soberly. 'My love.'

CHAPTER TEN

FOR the next three days she went around in a daze of love. It seemed as if Kosta would not let her out of his sight. They walked along the beach hand in hand. They got the generator going again together. They organised Kosta's work schedule together. They cooked and washed dishes and sat in silence together.

And they made love. Anywhere. Everywhere. Any time.

Annis would look up and see that intent look in his eyes. Her heart would beat hard and fast, her muscles would turn liquid, her skin would heat. And she would go to him. Once, in the middle of a late, lazy breakfast, they simply fell on each other and ended up, laughing and satiated, under the refectory table.

'You're wonderful,' said Kosta.

He sounded as if he meant it, thought Annis, marvelling.

There were only two things they did not do. They did not talk about his habit of sticking to the same woman for a maximum of a month. And they did not plan.

So, what? thought Annis. *I can't say I trust him and then start nit-picking. Either I do trust him or I don't. I've decided I do. So stop worrying.*

It was not difficult, living as she was in Kosta's uninhibited appreciation, sleeping in his arms. Even on the plane back Annis was still basking in bliss, despite the fact that she had said goodbye to Kosta in Naples.

'I've got to go back to Milan. Come with me,' he had urged, even when they'd been in the airport, standing in front of the screen that announced her departing flight.

Annis shook her head. 'I've promised Roy.'

'Do you always keep your promises?'

She kissed him lingeringly. She, who never kissed anyone in public.

'Always.'

His fingers closed on hers so hard she thought they would break. She knew the look in his eyes, too. If they had been in the kitchen at San Giorgio, instead of the concourse, they would have disappeared under the table. Annis drew a shaky breath.

He said harshly, 'Sit by your phone tonight.'

'I promise.'

She did too. But, by then, everything had changed.

It started when she got back to the flat. Annis ran through the messages on the machine and there were too many from Lynda, increasing in brevity and agitation as the days had gone by. Annis called her at once.

'Lynda, it's me. What's wrong? Has something happened to Dad?'

But it was not Tony. It was Bella. And Annis should have seen it coming.

'She says you've been away for the weekend with Kosta Vitale. Is it true?'

'Yes,' said Annis bewildered.

She could hear a sob in Lynda's voice, though she valiantly tried to suppress it.

'Oh, darling, don't let him break your heart like my poor Bella.'

'What?'

'I should never have let your father invite him to dinner. I knew Bella was interested. I even knew his reputation. He danced Jane Granger's daughter all round the maypole and then dumped her without any warning.'

Annis's lips felt anaesthetised. 'After a month.'

Lynda was trying to be sensible. 'Bella didn't even last that long. He took her out a couple of times. Then just stopped calling.'

Before or after he had taken Annis to bed? Annis wondered.

How long before he was going to tell her that he had been dating her sister? He had told her so much this weekend. He had said she would end up knowing everything about him. Would he ever have told her about Bella?

Why should he? said her inner voice nastily. He could have kept it quiet for another three-and-a-half weeks.

Lynda was saying mournfully, 'Bella usually weathers these things. It never occurred to me that she would be so hurt. Or that you—' She broke off.

'Would be the one to pinch her boyfriend,' supplied Annis.

This was going to hurt. It was going to hurt a *lot*. Any minute now, when she started to feel again.

'Oh, darling, don't think that. You weren't to know. She didn't tell anyone. She didn't tell me. A mother just picks up the signs.'

Annis pushed a mechanical hand through her hair. 'What do you want me to do? Talk to her? Not see him again?'

Lynda sighed. 'You can't hand a man round like a parcel. If he doesn't want Bella, whether you give him up or not isn't going to make any difference. I just don't want *you* to get hurt.'

Because, unlike Bella, you don't weather these things so well. Lynda did not say that, of course. But Annis knew it was what she meant. She thanked her in a suffocated voice and rang off.

She was sitting by the phone when he rang all right. Sitting and listening to his voice as he left a message. He even managed to sound disappointed.

'*Bastard*,' shouted Annis, throwing a coffee cup at the wall.

He called every hour. Then every half-hour. She still did not answer. By the end he was starting to sound alarmed.

So now he'll know how it feels for once, thought Annis.

She was at Vitale's at six-thirty the next morning. She worked like a whirlwind, hardly speaking to anyone, not eating, just inhaling black coffee and ploughing grimly on. Slightly to her surprise, Kosta did not call.

Maybe he was too busy. Or maybe he had lost interest already, she reasoned. Well, she was glad about that. Wasn't she?

She was utterly unprepared when he walked in at two o'clock. He was unshaven and with yellow shadows under his eyes. He marched into his office and banged the door behind him.

'What's going on?'

Annis jumped to her feet, suddenly deathly pale.

'Kosta!'

'Yes, that's me. The one you promised to be waiting for last night. Remember?'

Annis pulled herself together. She even managed to shrug. 'That was then.'

For a moment his expression was little short of murderous. 'I thought you kept your promises.'

She blinked. She had imagined their next meeting. In the last eighteen hours she had thought of little else. It had never once occurred to her in all that time that she would be in the wrong.

She said now furiously, 'Well, sorry about that, but I decided to cash in my chips.'

He was blank. 'What?'

'It was great ride. But I think I'll waive the next three-and-a-half weeks and go straight to the trash can now.'

'What the *hell* are you talking about?'

Annis gave an angry little laugh. 'Isn't it usually a month before you dump your women? I just thought I'd go before I was pushed.'

Kosta pushed a hand through his hair. 'What have you heard? Gossip? Why haven't you even *asked* me whether it's true?'

'Because I know it's true,' said Annis, icy calm. 'Don't forget I've read your e-mails. And my sister told me all about it before I realised you were the one she was talking about. When I did, of course, it all fell into place.'

'Your sister!' He looked thunderstruck. 'Bella? Am I supposed to have had a thing with Bella?'

'Didn't you?'

'Of course I didn't.'

'I don't believe you.'

'So what else is new?' he said grimly. 'What does a guy have to do to get you to trust him?'

Annis wanted to scream. 'Telling the truth would be a start.'

'I am telling the truth. Before your parents' dinner party I'd met her precisely four times. A party, a private view where Melissa ducked out and asked me to take Bella instead, once at a club, and once she turned up on my doorstep with champagne.' His voice was clipped. 'I've driven her home twice and kissed her once. I've never made a date with her and I've certainly never taken her to bed.'

Annis flinched. He saw it and his voice softened.

'Look, maybe she fancied me. I don't know about that. But I wouldn't have chased her. She's Tony Carew's daughter. I don't mix business with pleasure.'

Annis was scornful. 'I know that's a lie.'

In spite of the hard, anxious look, his mouth relaxed briefly. 'You are an exception to every rule I've ever given myself.'

She hardly heard that. 'But you couldn't take your eyes off her, could you? I saw you at my parents' dinner party.'

And she could still, only too clearly: Bella in her nightdress straps and short, swirling skirt, Kosta looking across the room at them, arrested and intent. She even knew what that intent look meant now. She could have wept. Instead she snarled, 'When Bella arrived you just stared and stared. Don't try and lie. I saw you.'

'Because I couldn't take my eyes off *you*.' He was exasperated. '*Think*. Who did I hunt down over coffee? Why would I do that if I weren't already going crazy over you? You'd told me comprehensively that you didn't date. You clearly meant it. And you also clearly didn't like me. What man would go looking for another poke in the eye if he could help himself? I couldn't.'

Annis did not believe him for a moment. That did not stop her wanting to believe him. 'Oh, you're so damned *plausible*,' she cried in despair.

He took her hands.

'Listen,' he said urgently. 'I broke every rule for you. I don't date millionaire's daughters. I don't date business connections. I don't have affairs with awkward, bad-tempered women who don't know how to play the game. And I don't take anyone to San Giorgio, date or not. Doesn't that tell the true story?'

Annis stared at him.

'From the moment I saw you at that party I haven't been able to get you out of my mind,' he said quietly. 'I never meant to start an affair. But from the moment I kissed you in the car—do you remember? You told me I needed civilising— I knew I'd met my match. I love you.'

Annis made an ugly sound of anguish.

'You'll stop at nothing, will you?' she whispered. Tears were pouring down her face. She did not even bother to dash them away. 'This isn't about love. This is about *winning*. Everyone knows you chase women until they give in and then you lose interest. I was a challenge, more of a difficult project than my poor Bella, so you chased me. And now you've got to get me back or you've lost the game.'

His head went back as if she had hit him. 'You don't mean that.'

But she did and he knew it.

She gathered up her belongings and put them into her briefcase. Her hands shook. They were very cold.

'Well, you can have your victory.' She blew her nose, not looking at him. 'I thought I was in love. I trusted you. You won. Well done.'

She snapped her briefcase shut and walked round the desk. Kosta barred her way. A muscle was working in his jaw and the green eyes were narrowed to dangerous slits.

'I'm going,' said Annis.

She was not afraid. He could not hurt her any more than he had done already, she thought.

She was wrong. He seized the briefcase away from her and flung it violently. Papers scattered as it bounced off the wall. But, by that time Annis was in his arms and he was kissing her as if he would devour her.

Terribly, her whole body convulsed with longing. Her hands even went to cradle his head, threading her fingers through that oh, so familiar hair. She knew him to the core, she knew his smell, the way his heart pumped when he wanted her—

Annis wrenched herself away. She could not bear it. She fled.

It was only out in the street that she realised she had left everything behind in the small purse she carried in her briefcase—cards, money, even her house keys. Well, she was not going to go back for anyone. She set out to walk home.

The Mayfair streets bustled with office workers coming back from late lunches. Fashionable women drifted in and out of discreetly luxurious shops. One or two of them glanced at Annis curiously. She realised that she still had tears on her face and dashed them away, furious with herself.

She had to go home. The porters had spare keys and she could walk to her block. It was only—what, four miles? And half of that through Hyde Park which, in all its golden autumnal glory, would be wonderful, Annis told herself firmly. She set a cracking pace and after a while the tears stopped.

She collected the keys and went wearily into the shower. She knew she had to ring Tracy and get her belongings back but, just for the moment, she could not face it.

The doorbell rang while she was just coming out of the shower. Annis hesitated. Would the porters have let Kosta in without ringing up to check that he was invited first? Surely not. But her heart was thundering painfully as she pulled her bathrobe tight up to her chin and cautiously opened the door.

'Oh,' she said, disappointed. 'It's you.'

'Where on earth have you been?' said Bella, marching in. She was holding a smart carrier bag and Annis's briefcase. 'I've been sitting downstairs with Gillie Larsen for hours. I was worried but she kept saying that you must have run away with a laser-tongued sex god.'

'Oh,' said Annis flushing. 'Well, I haven't.'

'No, I didn't think so,' agreed Bella grimly. She put her burdens down and surveyed Annis, hands on hips. 'You've been too busy listening to my mother.'

'Well, I—'

'You don't have to tell me. Kosta called.'

Annis flushed even harder.

'He *said* he wanted me to bring your case back. But what he meant was, how on earth could he get you to see sense?'

'I don't think what has gone on between Kosta and me is any of your business,' said Annis with dignity.

'It is if my daft mother has put a spanner in the works,' said Bella unanswerably.

She perched on the arm of a chair and met Annis's eyes, flushing faintly.

'Look, I had a crush on him, I suppose. I was piqued that he didn't take any notice of me. And then I saw what a really great guy he was. End of story.'

Annis stared. 'But you said you were in love,' she said slowly.

'I said I thought I was.' The tinge of pink deepened along Bella's perfect cheekbones. 'Heck what do I know about love? Anyway, he was never interested.'

'Never?' echoed Annis. Quite suddenly hope began to dawn.

Bella shook her head vigorously. 'Never. No matter how much I told myself this was a good sign or that was a good sign, he never even kissed me properly. I now realise he was only interested in you. I'm sorry I was too stupid to see it at the time. Like I said, what do I know about love?'

'Oh, Lord,' said Annis. 'What have I done?'

She sank down onto the sofa and dropped her head in her hands.

'I called him a liar. I said he was plausible.' She raised a tragic face. 'I said all he wanted was to win.'

Bella was rummaging in her bag. She produced a set of car keys. 'Then you'll have to grovel hard,' she said unsympathetically. 'Get dressed. I'm driving you over there.'

'Over where?'

'To Kosta's.'

Panic flared in Annis. 'I can't. I don't know where he lives.' The enormity of it struck her. 'I don't even know where he lives. We're complete strangers.'

'Complete strangers?' said Bella dryly. 'When you just spent an isolated weekend together? I don't think so. Come on. You're going to see him. And you're going to get him back.'

Annis stared at her in sudden suspicion. 'You mean, *you* know where Kosta lives?'

'Of course I do,' said Bella. She was patient but only just.

'I can't,' said Annis.

Bella had pulled black trousers and a lovely jewel crimson sweater out of her wardrobe, though the murals made her blink briefly.

'It must be like sleeping in the middle of a market place.'

'That's what Kosta said,' Annis remembered unwarily.

Bella stared at her. 'You let Kosta in *here*?'

Annis sniffed but she could not deny it.

Bella raised her eyes to heaven. 'How the hell can you say you are strangers? You're an ungrateful toad. Get dressed before I start throwing things.'

'What will I *say*?' wailed Annis.

But she knew, of course. Bella had told her weeks ago what the modern woman did to get her man. Annis had quailed then and she quailed now. But there was no other way. She was in the wrong and she had to put it right.

'Ring the bell,' said Bella, pushing her out of the car outside his prestigious Docklands block. She reached into the capacious carrier and handed Annis a bottle of champagne. 'Don't drop that.'

'But I—'

'When he opens the door you give it to him. You say, "I'm sorry. I love you. Please take me to bed."'

Annis hesitated, appalled.

'Go on,' said Bella briskly.

'I've never done anything like this. What if he won't listen?'

'You should have thought of that before you started throwing briefcases at him.'

'I didn't. He was the one who threw it.'

But remembering the passionate, uncontrolled kiss that had followed, Annis began to feel more hopeful. She clutched the champagne to her bosom, looped her bag over her shoulder and drew herself up to her full height.

'That's it, Brain Box. You can do it.' Bella blew her a kiss and slammed the passenger door shut. 'Just do me a favour? Get married quickly so I don't have to trip down the aisle after you in blue tulle.'

She drove off. Tears that she had been suppressing ever since Kosta's phone call streamed down her face. But Annis did not see them.

Annis was standing surrounded by box trees in terracotta pots with her head whirling. Get married? *Get married?*

As if she were in a dream she rang the entry phone and went in.

Kosta was waiting for her at the door of his apartment when she got out of the lift. He looked grave. He also looked exhausted. He still hadn't shaved, she saw.

Her heart turned over. Quite suddenly it did not take any courage at all.

She thrust the bottle of champagne at him.

'I'm sorry. I love you. Please take me to bed,' she recited, as Bella had instructed. And then, on her own initiative she added, 'I do trust you really. Or I wouldn't have let you see my Venetian fantasy. I just didn't *know* I did.'

He did not say anything. Over his shoulder she saw a huge

untidy room, full of golden wood and books, with a great movie screen of a window onto the river.

She thought, *He doesn't want me here.* Then she thought, *He'll never forgive me. And then, He's got someone here and I'm embarrassing him horribly.* She writhed at that thought. But as long as there was a chance, she could not bring herself to turn and go.

At last he said in a harsh voice, 'Do you really think I only care about winning?'

'No.'

'Do you believe I've never felt about a woman the way I feel about you?'

'I—I think so.'

'I'll prove it to you,' he said grimly, casting aside the champagne and swinging her off her feet.

Later, ages later, she shifted to remove the *Architectural Digest* from under her naked shoulder.

'Kosta?'

'Mmm?'

'I do trust you. I do. But who is the woman you share a car with in Sydney?'

Kosta gave a great shout of laughter and rolled them both out from under the piano.

'My mother. She uses my car as her runabout when I'm away. I go back about three times a year and repossess it. The rest of the time it's hers.'

'Oh. I knew it had to be something like that,' she assured him airily.

'Liar,' said Kosta. 'Love you when you're jealous.'

'I'm not jealous of your mother,' said Annis, revolted.

'My mother thinks I'm God.' He laughed, kissing her stomach. 'You'll be able to tell her she's wrong.'

Annis caught his hand and carried it to her breast. At once, in pure reflex, his fingers began to move deliciously, wickedly.

'I will indeed,' said Annis on a little gasp as she began to arch and tremble. 'I will indeed.'

EPILOGUE

Six months later they were on the beach below the castle. Kosta had been swimming but Annis was stretched out lazily under the little raffia-roofed hide-out he had built for her. The April sun was surprisingly warm and she gave a wriggle of appreciation.

'I love this place.'

Kosta was deeply tanned already. His green eyes glinted as he looked at her.

'I remember.'

They had made love here under the sun and under the stars. Her answering smile acknowledged it.

He sat down beside her and put a hand on her still flat stomach.

'Do you want me to keep the cove private? I can do it, you know. We own this bit of the shore. I can bar anyone else from using it if you want me to.'

Annis shook her head. 'No. We've made it our own in all the ways that count. I can share it with anyone else who is clever enough to find it.' She twined her fingers through his. 'Anyway, you don't believe in ownership.'

'I'm reconsidering,' Kosta admitted.

'*My* beach? *My* rocks?' she teased.

He bent and kissed her.

'*My* wife. *My* baby,' he corrected.

Annis sighed blissfully.

He kissed the fingers entwined with his. '*My* love,' he said.

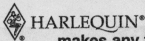

Harlequin Romance®